The

LEGEND

of

TOMMY
MORRIS

A Mystical Tale of Timeless Love

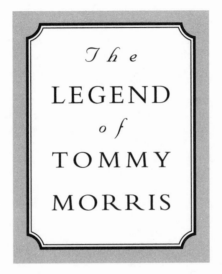

The
LEGEND
o f
TOMMY
MORRIS

ANNE KINSMAN FISHER

Based on the True Story of Golf's Greatest Champion

AMBER-ALLEN PUBLISHING ✦ SAN RAFAEL, CALIFORNIA

Amber-Allen Publishing, Inc.
P. O. Box 6657
San Rafael, CA 94903

Editorial and Production: Janet Mills
Printed by: R. R. Donnelley & Sons
Cover Design: Nita Ybarra Design
Cover Photo: Robert Tran

Library of Congress Cataloging-in-Publication Data

Fisher, Anne Kinsman, 1967–
The legend of Tommy Morris : a mystical tale of timeless love :
based on the true story of golf's greatest champion / Anne Kinsman Fisher.
p. cm. ISBN 1-878424-29-7 (cloth : acid-free paper)
1. Morris, Tommy, 1851-1875 — Fiction. 2. Golfers — Scotland — Fiction.
I. Title. PS3556.I7948L44 1996
813' .54 — dc20

96-23695 / CIP

ISBN 1-878424-29-7

First Printing October 1996
Printed in the U.S.A. on acid-free paper
Distributed by Publishers Group West

10   9   8   7   6   5   4   3   2   1

For Jeffrey

Remembering...I am with you

CONTENTS

1

ANCIENT MEMORY OF LOVE

TOMMY CAME TO ME AGAIN LAST NIGHT. I HAVE LONG SINCE realized I should not dream of a man who has been dead over a hundred years. But I've learned to welcome my visions of Tommy, for it was from his life that I learned the secret of love.

This was his legacy to me.

He lifted the blinders from my eyes to show me the way from desperation to love. He awakened my ancient memory of love and showed me how to touch the soul of another.

Love, Tommy told me, is the way our soul remembers its sacred connection to God.

Before Tommy, I was searching. I understood, without experience, how it would feel to have a connection so deep that it could heal the world. But I could never reach it.

What I thought would lead me to love had only led me farther away. There was no bridge from loneliness to love.

Looking back, I suppose I was led to Scotland not as an escape, but on a quest for answers. Scotland is a place that touches the heart. A place of misty highlands and timeless legends. A place where I could discover my own soul.

The answers came to me like a gradual fog lifting from the valley, hastened by the dawn.

I was in, of all places, a dusty Scottish bookstore when I found Tommy. Well, if truth be told, it was not Tommy I found at all, but his diary.

For me, it was an ordinary day — a day of sight-seeing and shopping. I was looking for golf books, rare books, anything to distract me from my despair. When you are longing for something you've never had, it is difficult to quiet the feeling. You know your life is not what it is meant to be, but the thought of what you want seems forever so elusive you're almost crushed by the desire.

Haunted by my own shadows, I was not prepared for the century-old diary I plucked from the crowded bookstacks.

Its worn leather binding was rubbed into a fine patina. The gilt edges of the pages were frayed. This book, I felt, had been much loved.

The paper crackled as I opened it to the last few handwritten pages.

November 16, 1875

Tell me, Jenny, how could you leave? Before we met, a part of me was empty. You brought the light with you. In your eyes, in your heart, I found what had been missing.

Love is everything, you once told me. It is all that really matters; it is all that really lasts. And yet I wonder . . . can I dare hope that love is, after all this pain, eternal?

Even the championships — how I laugh when others revere me for winning four Opens back to back. If they knew, as I do, how to illuminate every corner of life with love, they would see that anything is possible.

Teach me now, Jenny. Teach me how to reach you. You always said there were no boundaries to separate us. You never thought of death.

Everyone — my father included — says I am too inward now. Play golf, they say. Prepare for next year's Open. The grief will pass.

But they don't understand, do they, Jenny? They don't know what it is like to live in the light and then to be confined to darkness.

You came to me and showed me how to use my love to accomplish impossible goals. Now I will come to you. But can I will myself to cross the boundary? Can I will myself to die?

The pages snapped shut.

Whether I closed the book out of fear or shock, I do not know. At the time, I recognized only that I was deeply shaken. It was as if I had walked into the most private corners of a man's soul to eavesdrop. More disturbing, I found that his thoughts echoed my own. His longing, his desire for love, was the same as mine. This man, though, had apparently found the answer for which I was still searching.

I turned the book over and over in my hands, staring at it blindly.

"Put it back," I reasoned with myself. "You have no business reading someone else's diary."

Deep inside, though, I knew if I ignored this book, I would be running away from the very message I was seeking. In truth, it would be from cowardice and not a sense of propriety.

The war inside my head raged on for what seemed like

hours, but could only have been minutes. In the end, the lure of those handwritten pages was too much. They spoke to my heart in a language I could not resist.

2

THE FALLEN HERO

A COLD, FRAIL HAND GENTLY TAPPED MY SHOULDER. MY SKIN tingled as I visibly jumped and whirled around to face a soft, blue-eyed and white-haired old woman.

"I'm sorry, lassie. I startled you." She stated the fact plainly, without emotion. "We're about to close. You'll have to come back in the morning."

"Do you know whose diary this is?"

"Why that's a strange question for you to ask," she began, raising one eyebrow cautiously. "Of course I know. It's Young Tommy Morris'. He's a legend in St. Andrews, although not many people outside of Scotland know about him."

"What can you tell me about his life?"

She did not answer me right away; rather, she stared intently, first looking at me, then looking right through me. An otherworldly chill prickled my skin as I waited for her reply.

"Yes," she began slowly. "It is right to tell you.

"Young Tommy's life was brief, but all the more glorious because of what he discovered," she recounted. "Both triumph and tragedy were his companions."

With a mixture of pride and reverence, she declared that Tommy was the greatest golfer Scotland had ever seen. He had won four British Open tournaments — consecutively. No other golfer, before or since, had matched his record.

"The most amazing fact," she concluded, "is that Tommy accomplished this before the age of twenty-five."

" . . . and the tragedy?" I prompted.

Tommy was obviously a champion, but it was his sorrow that compelled me. From the diary, I could tell his pain and longing mirrored my own. What had he done about it?

"I want to know," I asked again.

"In that case" — the clerk nodded — "I suppose I should start at the beginning."

Young Tommy Morris, she told me, was the only son of

the head golf professional and greenskeeper at the famous Old Course at St. Andrews.

Tom Morris, Sr., nicknamed Old Tom to distinguish him from his son, bequeathed his passion for golf to Tommy. The two played countless golf "challenge matches" together, for there was only one formal tournament in the mid-nineteenth century, the British Open, so named because it was "open to the world."

In 1867, Old Tom Morris won the British Open at the age of forty-six. His victory was not a surprise, for Old Tom was the leading competitor for golf's most prestigious crown. He came back to defend his championship the following year, competing against his son, among others. By this time, Young Tommy was seventeen. He defeated not only his father, but everyone else to capture his first British Open title.

"There has never been a golfer since Tommy," she said, "who has understood golf as well — or life for that matter. Writers say he was a forceful player, creative and daring. But the reason for his success is not that complicated. It's simple. Tommy loved the game. He used that love to win."

Tommy won the Open in 1869 and again in 1870, becoming the first player in Scottish golfing history to win three back-to-back titles. His reward was permanent possession of the championship belt, crafted of red Moroccan leather, embroidered with silver medallions and encrusted with a single, perfect diamond.

When Young Tommy won his third championship in 1870, the tournament was scored over thirty-six holes. Tommy won by a margin of twelve strokes.

"Do you mean," I questioned, "his score was *twelve* strokes less than the nearest competitor?"

The arithmetic slowly dawned on me.

Today's golf tournaments are scored over seventy-two holes. Young Tommy had accomplished the equivalent of a twenty-four stroke lead.

It was unbelievable.

This young man was obviously one of the greatest players of the game. Why had I never heard of him before? Shouldn't his name be emblazoned with the best, a champion for each generation — Jack Nicklaus for today, Bobby Jones before him, leading all the way back . . . to Tommy?

"What happened to Tommy?" I urged her to continue.

"There was no Open in 1871," she laughed. "There was no prize. Tommy was in permanent possession of the coveted Moroccan belt. It took tournament organizers a full year to decide upon the new trophy, the current silver claret jug."

In typical Scottish prudence, the new jug would not be retired as the belt had. It would be entrusted to the champion's custody for a period of one year only. Never again would the British Open lose its trophy.

The following year, much to the chagrin of tournament organizers, Young Tommy won the Open again for an unprecedented fourth consecutive victory, a feat that has never been equaled.

The elderly clerk paused, a moment of silence seemingly in Tommy's honor.

She continued with a somber tone. "I suppose it is the grandeur of Tommy's success that makes the closing chapter all the more heartbreaking."

A few years after his 1872 victory, Young Tommy's wife went into labor with their first child.

A messenger interrupted Tommy's golf game to tell him that his wife was dangerously ill. The last train to St. Andrews had already left. He would have to wait until morning to know if his wife had lived through the night.

Heartsick, Tommy did not wait for the morning train. He borrowed a boat, fighting the tide to sail across the bay. Two hours later and weary with exhaustion, he stumbled out of the boat to receive the telegram telling him his wife was dead.

Three months later, on Christmas Eve, Young Tommy died.

He simply lay down in the bed he had shared with his beloved wife and died.

"The legend is," the old woman recounted, her eyes glistening with tears, "Tommy died of a broken heart."

3

A HAUNTING PRESENCE

I KNEW SOMETHING ABOUT BROKEN HEARTS. TWO THOUSAND miles from home, I had embarked upon a spiritual journey to heal my own heart.

I felt the need to audit the accounts of my life.

My work as a marketing consultant had been the center of my world for many years. But lately I had grown restless. The hours at work no longer passed effortlessly. It was hard to get started in the morning and too easy to leave in the afternoon.

I was beginning to question my sanity. I had once loved my work, but my heart was not in it anymore. There was a longing, a sadness about me that had not been there previously.

Time and again, I had tried to join my heart with another's. But all I had known were disastrous relationships with men to whom I meant too little, or for whom I had to sacrifice too much.

I wanted my life to have meaning. And, if I was bluntly honest with myself, I wanted my life to mean everything to someone else. I wanted a relationship that brought the kind of mind-bending happiness and unceasing joy I had only read about.

The question of how to find this was what brought me to Scotland.

So far, my journey had held no earth-shaking answers. With leisure moments to myself for the first time in years, I relaxed and enjoyed the beauty of the countryside.

"Perhaps my life is not too bad," I reasoned. I was neither miserable nor completely happy.

Certainly, I needed a vacation. Maybe this was exactly what life was about — exactly the lesson I was supposed to learn. Reality is not perfect happiness. Reality is working every day at a job for which I am skilled, being well-paid, and taking nice vacations.

"Life is about compromises," I thought. "Perhaps I should relax my standards for finding true love. After all, isn't it more important to find a man who can meet my basic needs than to hold out for someone who makes my heart leap?"

And so, with no travelling partner to please, I tried once again to quiet the voices in my heart and enjoy my time alone.

It almost worked.

I drove my rental car from one corner of the country to the other. I shared winding roads with sheep and ducks. I visited the craggy western coastline dotted with fishing boats anchored offshore. I passed through softly rolling mountains, one minute shrouded in rain, the next brightly lit in sun.

The weather in early September was much colder than I had anticipated. Each day, I wore the only sweater I had packed and delighted in cups of hot cocoa at breakfast.

I don't think I can pinpoint the precise moment it happened, but sometime in my winding journey across the country, the land began to weave a spell over me.

Scotland is a magical place. It is a land where the walls between spirit and reality are rubbed thin, where the world of the visible and the world of the invisible begin to intermingle.

Every hill, every field seemed to have a story to tell, a life as real and as tangible as my own. Centuries of love and loss and triumph were written across the scarred horizon.

Many years before I had learned to trust my intuition when travelling. In this way I found the simple, everyday treasures that add richness to a traveller's life. My friends called it luck; I called it following my heart — the silent intuition within my own soul. Either way, I was drawn to St. Andrews, tucked away on the eastern coast of Scotland.

I had developed a pattern of acquainting myself with a new town. I would browse through the city's center and follow the river, if there was one. In this way, I discovered many wonderful pubs, cozy bed-and-breakfasts, and eccentric shops.

Upon entering St. Andrews, I stuck to my habit and found as a result a weathered sign proclaiming *Rare and Not-So-Rare Books* hanging over a small street-front shop.

"The owner must have a sense of humor," I chuckled to myself as I went in.

Like used bookstores everywhere, this one smelled of decades-old dust. The shelves extended from floor to ceiling, crammed with books of every size and color. This was a place, I knew, where I could happily lose myself for hours.

The crowded shelves divided the store into tiny chambers. Winding left, then right, then left again, I came upon the shelf that held the diary of Tommy Morris.

Tracing the outline of the volume, I reluctantly handed it back to the clerk. "Thank you — for the story I mean. Tommy was" — I pondered — "an interesting man."

Speaking with intuition and wisdom, the clerk answered my unspoken question. "Young Tommy knew love is the only thing in this world that is not an illusion. Love is how he won the Open four times."

I stopped stark still, like a deer trapped in the headlights. I did not know how to react to this sudden intimacy. Her words struck to the core of my longing and the core of the dilemma that had brought me to Scotland.

I wanted to be loved. I wanted the kind of love Tommy had found. I longed to fulfill my heart's desires, just as Tommy had. It was as if this wrinkled bookstore clerk had seen into the secret corners of my soul. Her words echoed uncontrollably in my head: *Love is the only thing that is not an illusion. Love is how he won. . . . Love . . .*

"Stop," I silently willed myself. "Stop the words. Stop the longing."

Turning abruptly, I thrust the diary into her hands. I was dazed by her words. I had to get away. I murmured something about the day getting late and turned into the twilight outside the shop, digging my hands deep inside warm pockets.

Once outside, the compromise I had made to be neither truly happy nor truly miserable fell from the shelter of my intellect and shattered like shards of glass around my feet.

⁂

Some books, I believe, have a soul, and they long to share their story. Inevitably, they will open to just the page you're looking for.

Tommy's diary had touched me in this way. It was clear he had the answers to my questions. He knew how to tap the power of love to accomplish seemingly impossible goals. He had used love to become a golf champion, loving not only with his mind, but with his heart and soul.

Instinctively, I knew Tommy could teach me how to find true love.

The push and pull inside my heart was almost unbearable. "Don't leave Tommy's diary alone," my inner voice cried. "The answers are there."

And yet, I did not want the longing buried deep within me to surface. If I acknowledged how badly I wanted to be loved, how empty I felt, the feelings might overwhelm me.

Tommy's story raced through my body like an electric

current. Although I could not see its power, I could feel it.

Dreams of Tommy and his dead wife Jenny haunted my sleep that night. They were talking, looking out over a smooth green Scottish coastline. Jenny was speaking, but I couldn't hear her words. She took Tommy's hand with a tenderness that almost made me weep. She released his hand and swooped her arm across the sky, leaving a trail of diamonds sprinkled behind. I caught her words carried on the wind. "Love is all there is, Tommy."

I saw him winning the championship belt. One perfect diamond was removed and slipped on a band of gold to reside on Jenny's finger.

I saw Tommy at home, in the bed where they had shared so much love, his life slowly ebbing away.

My cheeks were damp with tears when I awoke. I knew sleep would not be forthcoming in these early morning hours, so I moved to the window seat of my room, bundled in my bed-quilt, and watched the sun rise.

My thoughts turned to myself.

I would follow this path. The answers would surely come

to me then. I would change my travel plans and stay in St. Andrews until I discovered the mystery Tommy's diary held for me.

My heart was turbulent, anxious, and excited all at once. My hands shook as I clutched the quilt around me tightly.

"Be calm," I told myself. "Breakfast will be ready in a few hours, and the bookstore will open soon after that."

4

Music of the Heart

THE OLD COWBELL TIED TO THE BOOKSTORE'S DOOR CLANGED obnoxiously as I swung it open. The elderly clerk said nothing; she merely nodded with recognition. The intimacy of the previous evening was gone.

I was left alone with my secrets.

I went in search of Tommy's.

I carefully wound my way through the bookstacks to the shelf that held the legacy of Tommy Morris.

As I clasped the diary in my hands and opened the pages, the veil between our two centuries lifted. I was no longer a reader, I was an observer. The scene was vivid in my mind's eye.

It was 1869. Tommy had already won his first Open championship.

He stood before the small looking-glass in his room, his hand running through his soft chestnut hair so like his mother's, which he wore unfashionably long. His eyes were his best feature. They were electric blue.

His body was lithe with broad shoulders and an easy grace. He had never spurted tall the way so many boys did at his age. Height was not in his family's genes. Bulk, it seemed, was not either. He was a well-conditioned athlete, lean and strong.

His hands, however, were golfer's hands. They were inordinately powerful, yet sensitive. When he grasped his putter, he could almost feel the ball sinking into the cup, such was his ability to control direction and speed. He had good hands.

I saw her again yesterday, walking along the beach, Tommy wrote in his diary.

The previous morning, like every morning he could remember, Tommy had visited his father at the Royal and Ancient Golf Club. Sometimes he and his father played their own private pattern of holes — never in the same order — but always adjoining the beach. Sometimes, Tommy played the holes alone, crafting his game. As he played that morning, Tommy spied her alone on the beach.

She was always alone, sometimes walking, sometimes staring at the sea. But she never seemed lonely. That was the peculiar part. Rather, she looked radiant, as if nothing in the world mattered but the beauty of her thoughts, the beauty of the beach. In fact, she seemed more a part of the beach itself than a separate human being.

Tommy was drawn to her as surely as he drew breath each day. For a time, he had been content to watch her silently, taking solace in the comfort and promise embodied by the slender figure on the beach. Now, as he gazed into the looking-glass, he ruthlessly appraised himself and hoped she would be pleased with his presence. He knew today would be their first introduction.

Tommy wrote in his diary: *I find it strange that my golf game has never been better since I first noticed her.*

What Tommy did not realize was that the dance had begun, the steps and gestures and music that bind one soul to another. In harmony, as if to a song only two could hear, the young woman walked the beach and Tommy played the golf course.

Their steps when they met would be in rhythm. He would

approach; she would say, "Hello, I've been waiting." Theirs was the path of two lovers destined to love. Like a series of doors that open only to the music of the heart, love is the passageway to the soul. It releases the power and the splendor trapped inside. One lover must hear the music and open the door, the other must step through.

The opportunity for such a love happens more often than we know. It is the destiny of all of us to become lovers. The music of love always plays; the doors are always ready to be opened. But how rare it is when two souls, in unison, hear the music and dance.

On that sunny April morning, Tommy's resolution to meet the young woman on the beach suddenly unsettled him. He was nervous. The forcefulness and dash that so intimidated other players on the golf course quickly evaporated once his clubs were packed away. Without a golf club in his hand, he felt naked and somehow inadequate.

Slowly, Tommy traced the route that would lead him to the Royal and Ancient Golf Club, through the narrow streets of St. Andrews, passing Tudor facades of century-old homes. As he faced the edge of the course, he looked out across the lush green wildness of the fairway, the North Sea stretching before him. The lone figure was there, as he knew she would be.

Resolutely, he took the first step across the dewy grass. Then another, and another, until his feet led him to the wide, sandy whiteness of the beach.

She was there, waiting for him.

As the two stood facing each other, the wind and waves created a spray, a spindrift, which misted between them, quietly insulating the pounding of Tommy's heart. Their meeting was not strained or awkward, but strangely familiar.

"My name is Jenny," she volunteered. "I've been watching you play. You're quite a remarkable golfer."

"I just play with all my heart," Tommy replied. "So far, it works. I win most matches."

"Then it must be your heart which is remarkable."

Tommy stopped.

He did not know how to respond. He could dismiss her words with a casual wit. Or he could let them penetrate his soul and in doing so would have to open himself in return.

The pause was palpable as Tommy considered what to do. His blue eyes were intense, gazing upon Jenny's soft features, taking in the essence of her. Her oval face was framed with a cloud of tangled curls the color of milky coffee. Her soft green-gray eyes were set just slightly too wide, and her chin was a shade too prominent, but somehow just right on her face.

Tommy heard the music.

"It's my father who is remarkable. He taught me how to play. But for me, golf is more than a game." Tommy took a quiet breath before revealing his secret distress. "My father is proud of me, of my talent, but I think he's also afraid of me."

The path was chosen. Tommy opened his heart.

The communion of their words, without limit and without reason, was now easy. The words that were always so hard for him to share longed for her company. They came effortlessly to him, spilling forth his heart's desires.

Tommy told her about his dreams for golf, how he wanted to win the championship belt as a talisman of his success, how he wanted to win the Open at least two more times in succession.

He told her about the raw powerful feeling of a wooden driver pummeling his golf ball farther than he had ever known a ball to fly. He told her how he often felt as if he were the one flying through the air, inside the ball, dropping to earth only when he found the exact spot he had envisioned.

Then, he told her about the arguments with his father, the demands his father had made that Tommy abandon his passion for golf and attend the university in St. Andrews. Tommy's golf, his father insisted, should be confined to the weekends to make room for an education.

"It's not my learnin' he wants to encourage. It's my golf he wants to stop." Tommy leaned forward, the resentment building to a crescendo within him.

He struggled to remain calm. "Jenny cannot possibly know how it feels to be denied the one thing that gives my life meaning — my golf," he thought.

In spite of himself, however, Tommy's steady blue gaze willed Jenny to respond.

She waited. The minutes passed and still she waited.

When her reply rolled gently into the air it cut to the heart of the matter. "Perhaps your father is feeling his age. He's just been beaten by his son in the greatest tournament in the world. In his eyes, a new generation is taking the lead, passing him by. Can you blame him for wanting to forestall the inevitable for a few more years?"

With these words, Jenny gave Tommy a rare glimpse into his father's soul. She had not judged who was right and who was wrong. She had not condemned Tommy for being angry. She had simply understood and spoken the truth. Tommy could well understand his father wanting to hold onto the power of victory. It was exactly how he himself felt about golf.

It was at this precise moment that Tommy fell in love. "Jenny, you have a rare gift for understanding."

"I know."

They were still, almost reverent in honor of the love that had sparked between them. Her face was hot from the intensity of the moment, as was his.

And then, just as suddenly as she had captured his heart, the mood was broken as Jenny whirled around and shouted, "Race you to the curve of the beach!"

They ran, and ran, until they both fell down in the sand, laughing and exhausted. And then, lying on their backs, they talked, not looking at each other, but looking at the wispy clouds overhead. They shared stories of family, of hopes, of sadness, and of love. When the words stopped, the silence was not loud as it so often is. The silence instead was comforting, soft and gentle like the lilt of Jenny's voice.

5

A Place Called Oneness

EVERY DAY THEREAFTER, JENNY WAS AT TOMMY'S SIDE AS HE practiced. Together, they traced the criss-cross of holes shadowing the beach. Tommy almost never played with his father anymore.

Most days, Tommy played the kind of championship golf that had won him his first Open title. Other days, however, he could not seem to make a connection with his clubs. But Tommy knew any slump would eventually be replaced with a win. Many times, he had seen his father play poorly and stomp off the golf course in frustration, only to play a challenge match the following day and win by five or more strokes.

Regardless of the quality of his play, Tommy took constant pleasure in Jenny's company. She was always there, encouraging, watching, praising.

"Tommy," she began as they stepped up to the tee of the sixth hole, "where do you go when you are winning a match? I can see it in your eyes, you are no longer here. You become so focused — as if nothing else exists, except you and this golf course."

Tommy stared at her, the recognition slowly dawning on his face. "You've just described exactly what happens to me."

He took Jenny's hand and led her to the slope of the green, where they sat. Their figures were framed by rough and tangled brambles. Every now and again Tommy would pause in the conversation to reach out and grab a branch, breaking the thorny stem in two.

"When I'm winning," he said, "I feel as if I've entered a special place where everything I do is preordained: the club I choose, the way I swing, where the ball lands. And when I reach this place, there is no other possible outcome but to win."

Tommy lowered his voice as if to make a confession. "Jenny, I believe this place is important not just in golf, but in life. It's a place where you know what you are meant to do, where there are no mistakes, no wrong choices, just a sense of joy in following your own heart."

He laughed softly. "Unfortunately, I can't always find the door to this place or remain there at will once it opens. I just know that when I'm in that special place, I always win. That's how I won the Open last year. That's how I hope to win again this year."

"I know this feeling you describe," Jenny said. "I've been there, too. It is a place where you connect with your soul, with the source of life itself. You go there to win a golf match, to prove yourself, to stretch your talent. I go there to escape from the pain in my life."

Jenny's voice faltered as she told him of the stories behind her pain, stories that broke Tommy's heart. It was the first time she had told these things to anyone.

Tears pricked unexpectedly behind Tommy's eyes.

He knew Jenny had grown up in a household without love. Perhaps there were too many children and too many demands upon her parents for them to take the time to love or acknowledge her.

But Tommy rather suspected that her parents, like so many people, did not want to bother with the tender yearnings of Jenny's heart. Everyone, it seemed, had a good excuse not to love.

He knew Jenny escaped to the beach whenever her family life became unbearable, but he had never felt her pain before, as he did now. It struck him as a white-hot sensation, lonely, terrifying. It was the pain of separation, of loving without being loved, of being connected to no one and to nothing in this world. At least Tommy had his golf.

Salty tears burned in Tommy's eyes as he held her in a steady gaze. "I see you as you truly are," he said simply. "In my eyes, you are lovely. I do not see your darkness, Jenny, I see its purpose in creating your beauty. Perhaps it is the darkness that enables you to radiate so much light. Holding you now is like holding a bit of heaven."

Tommy pulled her close. The air was still as they curled against each other and the alchemy of love worked its magic.

As Tommy saw only beauty within Jenny, the darkest corners of her heart were flooded with light. Jenny was finally loved.

"Can you tell me" — Tommy smiled a mischievous grin — "how to reach that special place where all is predestined, where there are no mistakes, no wrong choices, anytime I want? During a golf match, for example?"

Jenny nodded with amusement, knowing the love Tommy felt for her would soften his spirit and strengthen his golf game.

"What do you call it?" Tommy asked.

"Oneness."

⌘

Sitting there Indian-style on the bookstore floor, I closed the diary and began to think. I imagined how Tommy and Jenny felt, and my soul rang with the possibilities.

"Oneness," I thought, turning the word over and over in my mind like a talisman. "Is this how Tommy won his Open championships? Is this where love is found?"

Lost in my own thoughts, I was again startled by the elderly clerk. "It's closing time, dear."

"Can I borrow this diary?" I asked abruptly. "I don't really think you'd want to sell it."

The clerk looked puzzled for a moment, weighing an unspoken dilemma. Strangely, a glimmer of hope shone in her eyes.

She looked from my eager face to the leather-bound journal and back again. "I will ask the owner," she concluded, disappearing behind a storeroom door.

"What an odd woman," I muttered to myself as I turned my thoughts, inexorably, toward Tommy and Jenny.

Their last encounter was miraculous, I mused. Tommy felt her pain. He saw into her soul, saw all the raw and fearful feelings, and he loved her nonetheless. Like an alchemist, Tommy turned Jenny's pain into love. But her love transformed him also. Who gained more? Jenny or Tommy? The love that blossomed between them was balm for their souls, a power not of this earth, and yet one which could heal, completely, their wounds from this earth . . .

My reverie was broken by the clerk's return. "The owner's answer may not make sense to you now, but he was very specific. He says you may borrow the diary, of course, with one small request. You must return it to him personally."

"Thank you — or thank him." I laughed, wondering what the importance of his request could possibly be. "Let me leave my name and my hotel number with you, in case you need to be in touch with me."

"No. The owner was quite insistent on that point. He says he'll know you when you return."

"A strange reply, a strange experience," I thought silently, dismissing both the clerk and the bookstore owner with irritation.

I left the shop as quickly as I could, returning to my day-dreams about Tommy and Jenny.

6

ECHOES IN THE SAND

BRIGHT SUNLIGHT FILTERED THROUGH THE GAUZY CURTAINS of my room, waking me the next morning. It was my first day alone with Tommy.

A rush of anticipation soared through my heart as I remembered the diary was with me now. I could discover Tommy's secrets as quickly or as languidly as I pleased.

Looking at my nightstand, I saw the diary resting silently like an unopened present. I smiled with joyful suspense.

"This should be a special day," I thought to myself. "I should plan a celebration, perhaps a picnic at the beach, a day just like Tommy and Jenny must have shared."

Pushing back the bedcovers, I rose, grabbing my slacks, a long-sleeved shirt, and my much-worn sweater.

I kept a private cache of fruit, crackers, and bottled water in my room for late-night snacking. "Or for picnics," I laughed to myself as I stuffed my provisions into a daypack.

The beach bordered the golf course on all sides, I realized as I stood staring at the flat, wide expanse of sand and water. The wind whipped my hair forward to sting my face, and even though the temperature was no more than fifty degrees, I was pleasantly warmed by the sun.

Looking across my right shoulder, I saw the white marble outline of the Royal and Ancient Clubhouse. The golf course, now to my back, looped forward on the small jetty that comprised the Old Course. When I looked to my left, I saw a procession of silent golfers trekking across the green fairway.

"This must be what Jenny saw as she walked the beach every day," I imagined.

It was easy for me to feel her presence.

I closed my eyes to listen to the rush of the sea, the swirl of the wind. I felt the history, the timelessness of this beach. The sands crystallized beneath my feet, metamorphosing into the sands of a century before.

My face grew warm from the imagined heat of Tommy's gaze.

A smile ghosted across my lips as I turned my head, opening my eyes, expecting to see . . . Tommy.

Dazed, I looked straight out at the flat expanse of beach.

There was nothing there. Just endless sand stretching to infinity.

My thoughts pulled me onward.

"I can feel their love," I thought to myself. "It is here, on this beach, trapped inside the pockets of air."

I walked, one foot after another tracing Tommy and Jenny's steps. One pair of footprints in the sand unknowingly following the shadows, echoing the footprints from a century before.

My feelings swelled as I walked. They were almost tangible in my chest, beating with the rhythm of my heart. My breath caught in my throat from a sharp intake of excitement. "It was here they met. I know it."

I stopped, dropping my daypack to the sand.

I sat down slowly and unpacked the diary, running my hands over the worn leather binding. "Love is the answer, isn't it, Tommy?" I spoke aloud this time. "But is it the answer to golf, or to life?"

Opening the diary, I began to read. I smiled as I leaned back, scrunching my daypack behind my head. I quickly became engrossed in Tommy's story.

August 12, 1869

I would not have won my second Open championship if it weren't for Jenny. She shared her secret of oneness with me. She taught me how to reach that special place where there is only love . . . where I become inseparable from my desires and goals.

Love, she said, returns you to the knowledge of your soul, whereby your life becomes more purposeful, more meaningful, more eternal than you ever dared dream. Love empowers you to accomplish the impossible.

Jenny's wisdom came at just the right time. I was playing poorly as the tournament loomed near . . .

Closing my eyes, I felt the sun on my face, not from today, but from an early summer morning in 1869. Tommy and Jenny had been practicing, with very mixed results. The scene played in my mind.

"Damn it, Jenny." Tommy threw his club to the ground. "I can't make a connection with the course. I couldn't do it yesterday, or the day before. How will I ever win the Open?"

He turned from her in frustration, his hands tightly clenched. His fear was increasing with every hole he played, and he did not want her to see the naked terror in his eyes.

When he turned back to her, composed again, a faint smile crossed his lips. "Well, if I'm not meant to win the Open, I suppose I won't. Dreams aren't always attainable are they, Jenny?"

She looked at him wordlessly, deep into the blue of his eyes, into the blue of his heart.

"Tommy," she began in a soft lilt, "dreams are God's way of whispering to us. You cannot let this dream go, even if you are afraid." Jenny did not back away.

For an instant, anger flashed through Tommy's mind. Quit pushing, Jenny. Stop pressuring me. Don't you understand? I don't know if I can do it.

Fear was in control of him.

Tommy stared at her. His mouth opened to speak the words that would make her back away, angry words, fearful words. Instead, he was surprised by what escaped from his lips.

"I'm afraid." His heart, not his mind, had spoken.

Tears welled in his eyes. "I want to win this tournament so badly. Not for the glory, but because I am meant to win it.

This tournament is my destiny. I can feel it in every bone. But I don't know how to do it — how to leave my failure behind."

Jenny reached her hand to his cheek, cupping the curve of his face with elegant fingers.

"Use your love, Tommy."

"How?" he pleaded.

"The knowing is within you. You've done this before," she replied. "There are only two feelings in this world: love and fear. Love comes from God; it is real. Fear comes from our imagination; it is an illusion. Fear isn't real; it is man-made.

"Memories of past failure haunt us all. For you, every time you step up to the tee, you remember how it feels to hit a bad shot. For others, it is the pain of rejection, the shame of failure that haunts them.

"As long as you dwell on failure, you are not loving. As long as you forget to love, you are cut off from your power. Love transforms the past. It does not just make us feel better; it gives us a new outcome. When you come from a place of love, everything is possible."

"What can I do?" Tommy whispered.

"The secret is to release your fear and return to the memory of love."

"But my anger, my frustration . . ."

"Fear," she stated simply. "Call it what you will. Fear has many names, but in the end, it is still fear."

"To move beyond it," he asked, "to reach oneness, how do you do it?"

"Admit the fear first. It does no good to hide from it, or pretend it doesn't exist. Denial only gives fear power; it gives it more strength. I've learned to offer my fear to God, to ask him to heal it."

"And the love?" Tommy prompted.

"Without fear, the love will rush in to guide you. But you must consciously choose to love. You must intend to love this golf course, to love each shot. Your love, Tommy, is raw and powerful. It is pure. It will guide you."

Tommy stared at her. The simple truth of her words caught first in the mist, then in his mind, then in his heart. Determination took hold.

"Walk with me to the fifth hole," he asked.

Together, they approached the tee box. The fairway was no more than a hundred feet wide, a demanding strip that goaded a golfer to place the ball wisely or suffer punishment. Tommy teed his ball and looked at Jenny.

He spoke slowly. "Loving you, Jenny, has shown me the true nature of love. Until now, I thought your love had reached inside to touch my heart, that the magic came because I was loved. I was wrong. The magic comes because *I love*. The love must come from within me."

Tommy turned to his golf bag and selected a driver with a smooth wooden shaft. It was one his father had made for him. The power of love that had crafted the driver, the power of Jenny's presence, and Tommy's pure love for his game combined to create the most perfect golf the fifth hole at St. Andrews had ever seen.

Tommy positioned the club over the ball and looked over his left shoulder toward the flag on the green. The hole was 564 yards long, a par-five.

He decided to make this one in three shots, instead of the five allowed. He bent his head over the club.

Jenny watched him close his eyes and breathe deeply. She understood what Tommy was doing; he was bringing himself to that special place of oneness. In Tommy's head, he was praying, releasing his fear to God and visualizing each stroke that was to come. With Tommy's last exhale of breath, Jenny saw his shoulders relax.

He had wordlessly released his fear.

Eyes still closed, Tommy whispered, "I love you."

Jenny didn't know if he spoke to her or to the golf course.

The next few moments were magic. All sound, all wind, all feeling stopped.

All of nature held its breath in awe of Tommy.

His hands were decisively powerful. He waggled and swung the club. As it connected with the ball, the shaft snapped in two. The ball flew nearly three hundred yards, landing in the dead center of the fairway, just past seven hazardous bunkers.

Tommy did not notice the broken club. He walked resolutely toward his waiting ball.

His second shot landed close to the green, only twenty yards from the cup.

He selected his next club, a smooth-faced niblick, and positioned the ball almost off the tip of his right toe. His left toe pointed at the hole. He looked over his left shoulder, back down at the ball, and then he rapped the club against the ball.

It sunk into the cup. Three perfect shots from tee to hole. Tommy looked up, suddenly realizing that he was, after all, a separate being, and not a part of the golf course itself.

He took Jenny's hand and raised it to his lips. He pulled her close, his other arm circling her waist. His eyes never left hers; they were probing, direct, challenging. He bent his head and kissed her. Just before their lips met, he whispered, "I understand."

Tommy later won the 1869 British Open by a margin of three strokes.

༄

"I understand," I repeated as I closed the diary.

The secret Tommy had discovered on the fifth hole now struck me as well. Until this moment, I had not fathomed the source of love. I had always thought love would come from another, would strike my heart like a beacon and illuminate the dark corners. The prince would awaken me as the fairy tale had promised.

But love does not strike inward, Tommy had said. It comes from within and blossoms out. Love is already inside of us.

"So you have to love first," I mused.

That sounded very spiritual, a fine concept for Tommy to embrace in his golf, but not a very practical way of living. After all, the world had been a loveless place for me. It wouldn't be wise, I thought, to love someone who wasn't capable of loving me back, to expose myself to repeated rejection and abandonment. In today's world, you needed a strong ego to survive.

And then, strangely, in the midst of my disbelief, a thought erupted through my consciousness. It wasn't mine. It came from another heart, which seemed to be beating in tandem with mine.

It said, "Believe me, love is a very practical way of living."

"But how?" I wondered. "Is there enough love inside of me to reach out to another, as Tommy did? Or will my fear stand in the way like a mountain obscuring the sun?"

I was not sure I wanted to know the answer.

Tommy had confronted his fear on the golf course, but I quickly packed mine away in the darkest regions of my mind.

❧

I do not remember returning from the beach to my hotel that afternoon. I do not remember eating dinner, although I must have because I did not awake hungry for breakfast.

Rather, I awoke the next morning with tears staining my cheeks and with a hunger for Tommy's touch.

My first recollection of that morning was foggy, a memory or perhaps a dream suspended in the mist. I was not dreaming, nor was I fully awake. Perhaps I was where Tommy lived.

I felt the warmth of his body pressed against mine. He lay like a spoon behind me.

He was sleeping. I heard his soft, regular breathing, in and out. I had never felt so safe.

One arm was draped across my chest, the other circled under me, completely encasing my body. His cheek was warm against my hair. I felt exultant, protected, loved. This was where I belonged, in this man's arms. Here, I could be anything, do anything.

As he awoke, his hand stirred, caressing my breast. The instinctiveness of his touch was electrifying. He did not think to caress me, he simply moved with my body as if we were one.

I felt the calluses on his hands. I felt every nuance of his touch. His skin was rough, made hard and thick from a golf club grip. His touch, though, was tender. He was all power and strength, gently reined in to cup the heavy weight of my breast with infinite softness.

His lips drifted to my shoulder, his tongue tasting the salt of my skin. I felt him pressing against me, his arms pulling me tightly as leverage against the power of our union. I reached behind me, turning my head to open sleepy eyes to the face of my love.

He was gone. The other side of the bed was cold.

Tommy was not with me. It could not have been his hands stroking me. He was not my lover. Yet, his touch still lingered on my skin. The feeling of safety, of love, of wanting, still hung in the air.

If only I could fall asleep again, I thought. Perhaps I could recapture the dream. Perhaps I could traverse the bridge between now and eternity. Tommy would then hold me once again in his arms.

But I could not go back.

Waking consciousness was too much upon me.

I felt the cold sheets of the bed, the draft coming from under my hotel room door. I smelled breakfast cooking.

Tommy's touch had faded, yet I could still feel the memory of his love. He seemed to reach to me from across the boundaries of time.

Slowly, the realization crept upon me.

Tommy was becoming more than just the author of an ancient diary to me. He was becoming a real man, a man I could have loved, a man with whom I was falling in love.

Tommy opened the door to my heart, showing me how it felt to love and be loved. Out flowed my longing and desire; out flowed the tears I'd held back for so long.

Out flowed my fear.

7

RUNNING FROM DESTINY

I DESCENDED DEEPER INTO MADNESS EACH DAY, LOSING control of my thoughts and my emotions. For it surely must be madness to fall in love with a man whose bones have turned to ash.

I felt as if the insanity would swallow me.

I was bruised, stupefied by the feelings that had surged through my body. A thousand volts of electricity could not have jolted me more. After the dream, my knees were weak as I tried to rise from the bed.

My body ached. My eyes were puffy from too many tears.

I did not want anyone to look at my face. I wanted to hide.

I rubbed my eyes, shielding them with my hands.

"My life," I considered, "is a mockery of what God intended for me. He surely did not mean for me to always be on the outside looking in. He could not have meant for me to always be alone."

The emptiness engulfed me. My desire had been touched by Tommy, and for only an instant, it had been fulfilled. The rush, the magic, was incredible. It was everything I had imagined. The power of two souls joining together.

I had experienced oneness. But it was only a dream.

It was not real, and now the emptiness was more cavernous than before. The cold steel of my intellect formed the bars of my prison. Now that I knew what joy really was, I was left alone — again, as always.

I fought to maintain control, pushing aside the memory of love, hoping it would hurt less if I forgot how good it had felt.

"Stop longing for what you cannot have," I cried to myself. I feared that if I acknowledged the tidal flow of longing within me, I might never recover.

I stumbled to the shower, turning the hot water to full blast.

Hard rivulets of water pounded my naked body, pounding

out the feeling, blessedly erasing my emotions. I stood like a mute animal under the downpour until the water — and the echoes in my head — ran cold.

I dressed hurriedly, fearful that lingering would once again provoke my uneasy thoughts. I tied my hair back, leaving my face free of cosmetics, and donned a baseball cap. The typical American, I thought to myself. If I cannot hide physically, I can hide my eyes. I can hide the windows to my soul. I put on my sunglasses and left my hotel for a day of sight-seeing.

I knew, of course, where I would end up. The Royal and Ancient Golf Club. Tommy's club.

I entered the hall, quiet feet echoing on wooden floors. This was the hallowed ground of golf. I poked my head into room after room. It was dimly lit, smelling of leather and pipes like a Victorian gentleman's club. I looked into the Big Room where leather chairs circled around tiny cocktail tables. The walls were lined with lockers, small brass nameplates dusted over with age and disuse. A large portrait of Queen Elizabeth hung over the fireplace.

Stepping into the room, I walked to the window to overlook the first tee of the course. A small plaque on the window ledge noted that over forty thousand rounds of golf are played on the Old Course every year.

"One round, on this course, on this beginning tee, was played in 1869," I thought, "by Tommy Morris."

In the flat distance, I saw the fifth hole, the one Tommy had mastered with three strokes. How many golfers playing today, I wondered, would sink their ball in three strokes? No one today would likely equal the score of my century-old champion, for no one would play with his extraordinary love.

A chill ran through me.

I looked over my left shoulder, through the doorway to the room opposite the hallway. It appeared to be a Trophy Room. My feet moved toward it of their own accord.

Pictures lined the walls. Silver glistened from behind the cases. I saw the Calcutta Cup, made in India from melted-down rupees. I saw the Queen Victoria Jubilee vase, a relic from Victoria's twenty-fifth anniversary as sovereign. Behind me, though, was the lure.

My ears rang as if someone had called my name.

I fought the impulse to turn around as long as I possibly could, intently studying the scrollwork on Victoria's trophy

When I could stand it no longer, I turned, and stared. There, on the opposite wall, was a simple red Moroccan leather belt encased in glass. I approached, reading the plaque underneath.

Tom Morris, Jr. won permanent possession of this belt, the original trophy of the British Open, by winning three consecutive tournaments in 1868, 1869, and 1870. The belt was donated to the Club after Young Tom's death in 1875.

I was hypnotized by the belt.

I looked at it, at the red grainy leather. The silver medallions sparkled as if polished only yesterday. There, in the center of the belt, was a worn spot. There were gashes in the leather, as if some type of ornament had once been held there.

I looked at the gashes quizzically.

"Jenny's diamond!" The words came from my lips, but somehow not from me.

My hand flew to my mouth as if I could catch the words and force them back inside. How did I know there had once been a diamond in the center of the belt? There was no mention of a diamond on the plaque. I had not read of a diamond in the diary. There was only . . . my dream.

"My God," I gasped. "No. It can't be."

The blackness swirled before me.

And then, Tommy spoke. His voice was deep and melodious in my head, unbidden by the diary.

"Love can accomplish the impossible," he said.

His voice rushed through me. "Love is the only thing that is real, the only thing that lasts. This belt is my legacy, my testament to love. It is here on this wall for all who have eyes to see. You can feel its power, as Jenny and I did. Surrender to love."

I began to shake.

Here, in front of me, was proof— actual, tangible proof— that my dreams were real. I was divining Tommy's presence, calling him and Jenny, and their love, back to me.

I could not stop shaking.

"I do not want this," I said with more conviction than I felt. My eyes welled with tears. "Do you hear me, Tommy? Not if I have to be turned inside out."

I turned resolutely and left the club. Each step echoed, taking me one by one farther away from Tommy.

As I reached the bottom stair, I began to run.

I will push these thoughts out, I told myself. I will push out the longing; I will push out the madness. I will push it deep inside until there is no place left for it to go.

8

BEYOND THE RUINS

BY THE NEXT MORNING, I HAD REACHED A COMPROMISE WITH myself. The raw, naked fear that had so unnerved me was quiet now. I had successfully outrun it. I was able to shove it inside its box once more. I closed and locked the lid.

I felt almost safe again, and I resolved to spend a day or two away from the diary.

"I won't ignore it altogether," I reasoned. "After all, I do want to learn Tommy's secrets. I just want to learn them in my own time."

I spent the morning poring over tourist brochures.

St. Andrews, I learned, was not just the center of golfing history. Religious pilgrims travelled here looking for a miracle. They journeyed from across Europe to pray before the relics of the shrine of the St. Andrews Cathedral.

Mary Queen of Scots, a favorite Scottish heroine, had also worshipped at the cathedral. She had considered St. Andrews to be the most beautiful city in her kingdom and had spent much of her brief life here, enjoying the golf and the seaside air. The ghost of her second husband, Lord Darnley, was believed to make appearances from time to time at the cathedral ruins.

I should have had my fill of ghosts, but the brief mention of Lord Darnley and of pilgrims searching for miracles was enough to pique my interest.

"I will visit the cathedral ruins today," I decided.

It was raining as I set out. A misty rain really, just enough to dampen the air, causing my hair to go limp with the humidity.

As I reached the ruins, I saw, looming over them, the Tower of St. Rule. The gray stone tower was set on a foundation of boulders. It was the only complete structure left standing.

There were steps and guardrailings for tourists, and I climbed to the top as the wind whistled across the damp stairs.

It was eerie — the gray and misty sky, the lonely stone ruins, pigeons cooing in the distance.

At the top, I looked across the far side of the tower. "There are no mysteries here, just a beautiful view," I thought confidently. I could see the Lomond Hills of Fife, green and rolling in the distance. The hills were smaller, somehow softer, than the rugged mountains of the Highlands.

I turned to the view at the back of the tower, to see the cathedral ruins themselves. Looking down, my breath caught in my throat. It was a sheer drop to the remains.

The cathedral, once lovely with graceful arches and carved stones, now lay spoiled and ravaged on the grass. The ground seemed to rush toward me as I looked steadily downward. A wave of vertigo hit me.

I grabbed the railing to steady myself, but I could not tear my eyes away from the sight of the ruined cathedral.

Forms materialized on the grass below.

A young man, old-fashioned in knee breeches.

A woman whose tangled curls were caught at the nape of her neck with a broad blue ribbon.

It was Tommy and Jenny.

Tommy held her hand, leading her to sit on a smooth boulder. He knelt before her, pulling back his waistcoat to reveal the red leather belt. Their voices were carried to me on the wind. "This diamond, Jenny" — he pointed to the center stone, which sparkled from the sunlight of another era — "this will be your engagement ring. Will you be my wife?"

Her eyes were bright. Words were unnecessary. She spoke with the language of love.

She rose, standing tall above him as he knelt. She touched his shoulder and traced the outline of his neck, then his cheek, gently lifting his face to meet her dawning smile. She held her hand out for his.

Tommy slowly rose to his feet, his eyes never leaving hers. Jenny released his hand, and they stood for an instant not touching but somehow closer than ever. She reached to cup his face in her hands and kissed him, slowly at first, then passionately.

Tommy thrust both arms around her waist, pulling her tightly to him. He lifted her and swung her around and around. Jenny's long skirts swirled in the air, her head flung back with laughter.

The sound of their laughter, joyous and bright, rang in my ears.

Tommy whispered to Jenny, but it was I who heard him. "Love is the way our soul remembers its sacred connection to

God. Love is an ancient memory that must be awakened within us. It is the means by which the invisible, our dreams, become visible."

As Tommy swirled his lover, he looked up.

His eyes locked with mine. They were the most beautiful shade of blue I had ever seen.

Slowly, the vision began to fade.

I released the guardrailing from my grasp, turning to sink to the floor. I sat there, knees close to my chest.

There was no turning back, I now knew.

Tommy and Jenny were coming to me without reading the diary. I was no longer in control. Perhaps it was an illusion that I ever was.

"Their love did not die," I realized. "They left it here for me to discover. They left it for anyone who has eyes to see beyond the ruins."

9

My Heart's Desire

SURRENDER WAS EASY ONCE I ACCEPTED THAT I REALLY HAD NO choice. I now knew I could not control my visions of Tommy and Jenny.

In the end, I could not control love. It would come to me of its own accord, unfold to me in its own time.

"It's funny," I laughed to myself, "I have spent so many years searching for love, longing for love. But when it finally comes to me through Tommy — when at last I feel the kind of love that touches my soul and opens my heart — the first thing I do is run from it."

I wondered if I had been running from love for years.

Was I, who had always wanted a man to love me completely, able to love another as completely as Tommy loved Jenny? Was I capable of giving the love I had demanded of others?

I was embarrassed by the answer. I had believed that loving was simple and finding the right man was difficult. I had spent so many years praying for the right man to come into my life.

I had been praying for the wrong thing.

I should have prayed that I become the right woman, that the blinders be removed from my eyes so I could see the love that was already inside me. Love is our natural state — that is why we long to return to it.

I would surrender to love and let down the barriers.

"Thank you, Tommy," I silently mouthed as I left the cathedral ruins. "I am no longer blind."

⌘

The rest of Tommy's story came easily to me. I savored the feelings and the intuitions, which slowly unfolded.

I resolved to trace Tommy's steps through the town of

St. Andrews. I wanted to eat where he ate, walk where he walked. I wanted to open my heart to Tommy's presence.

Late that afternoon, I lunched at the Jigger Inn, the oldest pub in town. I sat at a smooth, round mahogany table with my back to the wall. Butter yellow walls surrounded me, bearing photographs and golfing pictures from various eras.

My heart lurched as I looked up and saw, hanging on the wall to my right, a picture of Tommy. It was a formal photograph; Tommy's waistcoat was open, displaying his championship belt. "Spooky," I thought, as he seemed to be watching me study the menu.

I ordered fish and chips, with a half-pint of stout ale. It was a Scottish lunch. The type of lunch Tommy once ate, I suspected. As I broke the fish apart to eat it, tender chunks of fried batter dropped into the paper basket. I quickly gulped the steaming hot fish and grabbed my beer to quench the heat. It was surprisingly bitter.

Leaving a pound coin as a tip, I paid my bill and left, wondering where Tommy would go after lunch.

"The golf course," I concluded.

Evening was approaching. The sky, so gray and misty earlier, was now clearing. Wisps of clouds streaked the colors of twilight, making the sunset all the more brilliant. The colors of this St. Andrews sky were deep coral and crimson red, stretching into mulberry.

I walked the short block to the edge of the Old Course, crossing the street to approach the fairway. I entered by the gate that bound the far edge of the course and stopped just inside the white railings.

Leaning against the wooden fence, I took in the sight of the deepening sunset and the surf in the distance. I watched as a final group of golfers crossed the famous Swilcan stone bridge, silently making their way toward the eighteenth green.

Two of the men walked together, deep in conversation. One was an old man with a long white beard, dressed in old-fashioned tweeds. His companion was younger, his strides long and determined. Brown waves of hair curled at the edge of his collar, and when he lifted his head, I saw Tommy's brilliant blue eyes.

"I will not stop you from coming to me now," I said aloud. I stood there, in the darkening light, transfixed by the sight of Tommy's approach. I waited at the white railing, unable to move, until the sky grew inky purple behind me.

The sun passed behind the horizon just as Tommy sank his final putt on the eighteenth green. Then he disappeared. His body grew misty, particles of eternity returning to their invisible form.

I felt the cold air wrap around me. I could no longer wait outside in the chilling darkness for Tommy. But I knew with the sureness of a lover that he would come.

I had invited him in. He would follow.

I returned to my hotel, took a hot shower, and snuggled into bed. I was calmer and happier than I had been in years. The hesitation, the fear of the previous days had lifted.

I reached for the diary.

"Teach me what I need to learn," I said as I opened the cover and began to read.

May 4, 1872

Forgiveness does not heal the heart of another so much as it opens your own heart to love. My resentments toward Father have festered inside me for years. His compliments have been few, his criticisms many.

To forgive him for pushing me to live his vision, rather than my own, has been difficult. But I have to root out this hardness in my heart, to make room for more love.

I naively thought I could love Jenny, love my golf, and still resent Father. But love is a power which demands every corner of your life . . .

I turned the diary page and began to imagine the scenes Tommy described, the scenes of father and son playing golf together, discussing the future.

It was early 1872.

"Young Tommy," the old man wheezed, "what do you mean you won't compete for the Open trophy again this year? Are ye daft?"

"Father" — Tommy grew more exasperated by the moment — "I have told you. Jenny and I are marrying. Our life together is the most important thing to me. I can play anytime — and I do. I earn plenty of money playing challenge matches. I just don't feel the need to play the Open again."

"Daft." Old Tom spit the word out. "I knew this would happen if ye didna go to University. It's been too much success, too soon."

"Father, listen to me." Tommy's words became rough. "I play golf whenever I wish. I don't need to compete in the Open again."

Old Tom snorted. He turned from Tommy, briskly made

his tee shot, and began to walk toward the waiting ball.

Tommy did not even have time to hit his own ball. He hurried to catch up with his father.

As Old Tom approached his ball, he paused. Never turning to look at Tommy, he spoke from memory.

"I took ye to your first tournament in Perth at age thirteen. You won fifteen pounds by beating the young Greig boy. I could see your genius then. Why d'ye think I refused your pleas to play in public again for three more years? So ye could practice, so ye could hone your game without the distracting glare of adoration.

"Then, when you were sixteen, I took ye to Carnoustie. It's the strongest course in Scotland. You were up against the best players. Do you know that Willie Park chided me when he saw you? He asked, 'What have ye brought the laddie for, Tom?'

" 'Ye'll know what for soon enough,' I answered him.

"And he did. Ye tied Willie Park for first place, and then beat him in a play-off. At seventeen you beat *me* for the Open title. Ye won it again, and again. Now, you tell me ye don't need to compete.

"Compete for me, Tommy. Compete for me," he said.

Old Tom was silent now. Tommy felt the charged emotions.

The hurt, the betrayal, and the jealousy hung almost palpably in the air.

The hair on Tommy's arms rose. His face flushed as his mind filled with angry thoughts.

Tommy stood still, his mouth closed. Instead of speaking, he listened to his inner voice, which cried, "How dare you make me feel guilty for not competing! It is *my* talent, not yours. Why can't you understand I have accomplished my mission and it is time now to explore my life with Jenny? How can you be my father and understand so little about me?"

Tommy clenched his jaw. But just as he was about to give voice to the angry thoughts in his head, Old Tom turned around, his eyes wet with tears.

Tommy had never seen his father cry. Now the old man was spilling over with emotion.

Tommy's jaw unclenched; the tension poured out of his body. He realized he could not condemn this man, nor could he speak in anger. Perhaps his father really did love him.

Tommy placed his hand on his father's shoulder and asked the question that had burned in his soul for so long. "Do you love me, Father?"

"What do you think I've been trying to tell you? I could cope wi' the others. I could cope wi' Allen Robertson, wi'

Willie Park, and the other great golfers. But I could never cope wi' you, Tommy. I never knew what to do. Of course ye are dear to my heart."

Suddenly, finally, Tommy understood.

There was nothing, really, for him to forgive. His father loved him; he had done his best to nurture Tommy's talent. Old Tom had reached the limits of his understanding. His love for Tommy had always been there; it was simply not expressed in a way that Tommy could understand.

Tommy considered what he should do.

Trying to make his father understand his motivations seemed to be a losing proposition. They always argued over who was right and who was wrong.

Then, it came to him.

Rather than react with anger — with harsh words or harsh actions — he would focus on the love between them.

"All right, Father," Tommy began slowly. "I inherited my talent from you, and you have taught me well. I know you have done your best. I will play a last round of competitive golf in this year's Open tournament in your honor. We will play together, and I will win it for you. Then I shall retire."

Old Tom softened, his eyes still bright.

"To play golf wi' you, Tommy, is the greatest joy of my life."

10

THE LANGUAGE OF HEAVEN

RELEASING THE LOVE INSIDE HIS HEART REVEALED THE
language of heaven to Tommy. He forgave his father, he forgave every pettiness that hurt him. There was no room in his
heart to harbor anger or pain. There was only room for love.

It was a crisp, white December day when Tommy opened
his diary again. He sat in a small room with frosted glass windows facing out toward a broad sea inlet.

It was Christmas 1874, Tommy and Jenny's first Christmas
together as husband and wife. A young fir tree was decorated
with popcorn, candles, and red velvet bows. There, in the glow

of the Christmas candles, Tommy raised his quill pen.

December 21, 1874

>   *I have come to realize the importance of choosing to see the divinity in other people instead of their limitations. Where there is divinity, there is love. Where there is love, there can be no conflict. . . .*

>   *Perhaps this is my life's mission: to teach others that love is not just a feeling, but a way of living.*

Tommy stilled his pen, lost in thought. His life with Jenny had become a full expression of their love. With a pureness of spirit, their love flowed ever deeper until there was now one soul where there once had been two.

Tommy cherished every word Jenny had spoken, every moment they had shared.

Slowly he traced the outline of the gift in his pocket, purchased for Jenny earlier that day. He wondered when she would return.

"It must be soon," he thought. "Her appointment was for three o'clock. She should be home by now."

Tommy looked at his watch to confirm the time. It was

only three-thirty. He laughed. Time without Jenny passed slowly indeed.

Tommy closed his diary, casting his eyes toward the fragrant Christmas tree. Mesmerized by the sight of the tree Jenny had decorated, Tommy reflected on the events that had led to this moment.

He still played golf almost every day, but after the 1872 Open he did not play competitively anymore.

Tommy had transcended his need for achievement. He gave the gift of golf back to other players, players who had not yet discovered how to use love to win.

"It would not be fair," Tommy laughed as he remembered, "to win every Open tournament. I'll leave a few for the others."

Tommy still used his skill on the golf course, though. He played for enjoyment, and he played to earn a living for himself and Jenny.

He attacked the pockets of every golfer who ventured to bet against him. His reputation for daring and skill won him not only exciting challenge matches but also huge profits, as foolhardy gamblers vied to beat the great Young Tommy Morris.

Tommy remembered a day several months before he and

Jenny had been married, a day that forever defined the priorities of his life.

He had been playing a challenge match against another golfer. He could not now remember the man's name. It was not important. Tommy was winning, as always.

He was on the eighteenth hole of the Old Course. His ball lay only four feet from the cup. Tommy carefully positioned his club behind the ball, quietly focusing on the task before him. Tommy always took great pains with his short putts, knowing that many players became too confident, and lost matches with sloppy putting.

Just as he pulled his club back to strike the ball, the hair on Tommy's neck bristled.

He looked up.

There on the edge of the green stood Jenny.

Though she often came to watch him play, he never tired of seeing her soft countenance. It was always like the first time. His heart rose in his chest. He did not want to take his eyes from the beauty of her face.

He looked back at his golfing partner and laughed. The man was ten strokes behind.

Tommy shook his head and sank the putt.

"Leave my winnings with my father," Tommy shouted as

he walked toward Jenny. "The golf does not matter now," he whispered to himself. "Jenny's here."

He approached slowly and took Jenny's hands in his own, breathing in her presence.

"How I love you, Tommy Morris," she beamed. "Do you know how you look before you realize I am here? You're intent, blind to anything in the world but your golf ball. There are beautiful little furrows between your eyebrows." She lifted her finger, gently tracing the smooth skin that, just a moment before, had been clenched in concentration.

"And then," she continued, "I can see the feeling — the feeling of me — go through your body. You turn and look up with the most beatific smile — as if you are seeing creation for the first time. All the beginnings and all the endings the world has ever known are in that one look. It is then that I know how much you love me."

They were like the moon and earth orbiting each other, he thought. It had always been that way.

They affected each other; they pulled each other. Sometimes, they came so close, two beautiful and perfect spheres, it seemed as if their power would explode. Then they would separate again, moving from night into day, to trace separate journeys and rejoin again.

Tommy remembered something he had written in his diary shortly before their wedding: *There is a higher purpose, a perfect plan for our lives. Each step we take, whether we recognize it or not, is leading us toward this purpose, this perfection.*

The sky that evening was ominous, steely grey with dark billowing clouds. It was a night to stay indoors, but Jenny had been insistent. She had found a house she wanted Tommy to see. It was a house, she said, that had been loved before, a house that would hold their love, too.

The house looked out upon a magnificent view of the beach. Just outside St. Andrews, it was tucked on a remote jetty accessed by a winding, one-lane sand road.

The estuary road twisted as Tommy and Jenny approached the house, leading them between sand dunes and drifts of tall grass. Then, the road widened to reveal a small, whitewashed stucco cottage.

The windows were handblown, uneven patterns of glass reflecting in the light. A large window faced the road, and looking through it, Tommy saw another window on the opposite side facing the beach.

Yes, he thought, Jenny was right. Love was here.

Jenny took his hand and led him through the curved, wooden front door. She showed him every room and told him of her dreams: a nursery for their children, a garden for out-side picnics, a Christmas tree placed near the window and lighted for all who would approach from the road.

This was already their home, he realized. It was waiting for them.

Jenny led Tommy outside, pulling him forward with her excitement, to see the view of the beach from behind the house.

It was then that the skies opened.

The dark clouds grew instantly angry, colliding with one another. The ocean churned, foaming and crashing against the beach.

Tommy and Jenny stood transfixed by the power of nature. A streak of lightning, raw and electric, jetted far in the distance. Two, three, four seconds later, they heard the crash. Booming energy shook the ground.

They could not move.

Standing there, behind the house, they were soaked by the rain. The winds howled across the open beach, and still they could not move.

Jenny, her body slightly in front of Tommy's, reached out her hand. Tommy grasped it, and they stood with only their hands touching, in witness to the raw majesty of the storm.

"This is God's voice," Jenny breathed. "Beautiful, electric, sometimes peaceful and sometimes fierce. Nature is God's voice."

Tommy felt the storm raging all around them, and he understood. The pelting rain which stung his face would, in the process, cleanse the earth. Just as the storm was unpredictable, mysterious, fearsome — so was life.

"We are here for a purpose," Tommy said, his thoughts an extension of Jenny's own. "We may not understand what it is, but there is always a higher will."

With this experience, their souls were joined as surely as the storm drenched the earth. The magic of that night stayed with Tommy forever, another memory to be relived, another connection to bind him to Jenny.

Tommy thought of their wedding. Jenny had been such a beautiful bride, carrying bunches of heather in her arms.

Everyone had come to the wedding — dignitaries, golfing heroes, and friends alike. The chief justice of Scotland himself, Tommy's frequent playing partner, had performed the ceremony.

Another friend brought confetti to the church to throw as Tommy and Jenny exited through the gauntlet of admirers.

Long strands of curling paper were tossed at them like

trajectories catapulting toward their prey. Tommy and Jenny ran toward the waiting carriage, cheers and laughter receding behind them. They collapsed, laughing and exhausted, onto the seat.

As the carriage pulled away, Tommy looked over at Jenny. She was pulling the confetti from her hair, leaning over to sweep the strands from Tommy's shoulders.

He marveled at the sight of his new bride, glowing as brightly as the noontime sun. Clouds of ivory tulle floated behind her, pulled back by a brilliant tiara.

One lone strand of confetti remained safe from Jenny's ministrations. It coiled from behind her neck to drape over her shoulder.

Tommy looked intently at Jenny, locking her eyes, stilling her movement. He lifted his hand to grasp the end of the confetti strand, pulling it slowly from Jenny's skin. The curled paper etched electrically across her skin, as surely as if his finger had traced the outline of her breast.

Tommy brushed the hair from her face, curving his hand around her cheek.

He bent closer and whispered, "My wife."

In an instant, Tommy knew they had always been joined in spirit. Their spirits were not confined to their bodies; their spirits were not confined in time. They were joined as one, and they would always be together.

࿓

Tommy looked at his watch again, jarring himself from the sweetness of his daydreams. He wondered, sleepily, why Jenny was so late.

He leaned his head back on the couch, letting the warmth of their home, the warmth of the Christmas tree, lull him into sleep.

As Jenny opened the front door, she saw her husband slumped low on the couch, his feet kicked out in front of him, arms resting motionless across his chest.

Jenny stood for a moment, in awe of the raw power that was now at rest in the body of Tommy Morris.

She sat beside him, to watch him sleep.

His hair curled back from his face, one tendril escaping to drape across his forehead. His hands, so often clenched in concentration, were soft and motionless. His brow was smooth. Long, silky eyelashes rested on his cheeks.

Jenny could see the boy that still lived inside the man, and her heart filled with love.

She raised her arm, tenderly, across the back of the couch to stroke his hair. She could not keep herself from touching him.

Slowly, in response to her tenderness, Tommy opened his eyes. His power, once silent in sleep, now slowly poured back into his body.

"You're home," he murmured, reaching to pull her near. "Do you know? Is it true?"

Jenny's smile answered him with full promise. "Yes, Tommy. We're going to have a baby."

"My beautiful, beautiful Jenny," he breathed, looping one hand around her waist, the other tangled in her hair. "Our life, our love, is expanding. First there was only you, then the two of us together; now there will be three. We are bringing a new life into existence."

Every detail of this moment — her scent, the feel of her in his arms, the rapture in his heart — was burned into his memory.

He remembered the waiting gift. Reaching into his pocket, he extracted a three-inch square packet of heavy white tissue paper.

"For you, for the babe," Tommy declared as he plopped the packet into her lap.

Jenny fingered it, heavy in her hands, and pulled back the tissue to reveal a cobalt blue blown-glass suncatcher. A brilliant sun was etched in the center, exactly where the sun's rays would reflect its blue brilliance.

She was speechless at the beauty of his unexpected gift.

Tommy spoke first. "It is so our child will always look for the light and know that from the light comes love."

"Oh, Tommy," Jenny sighed, the emotion catching in her voice. "I have never been so happy."

11

A Death in St. Andrews

I AWOKE THE NEXT MORNING TO COMPLETE AND UTTER BLISS, the diary still in my hands. Tommy and Jenny were married. They had built a life together.

Their happiness radiated from Tommy's diary as I clutched it to my chest. Together, the diary and I snuggled into the warm goose-down quilt of my bed.

The lessons of love were coming so quickly now, it was dizzying. I absorbed every page of the diary, every scene of happiness.

My soul was, at last, being fed.

Tommy and Jenny had found the secret of love. They had somehow created a life built with love, and I wanted to know every detail. Their fulfillment was my freedom — freedom from the past, freedom from the pain, freedom from the longing for love.

I closed my eyes to recapture my visions of Tommy and Jenny.

I saw their home, the nursery, the cobalt blue suncatcher suspended in the window above the baby's cradle. Jenny sat in an old-fashioned wooden rocker, swaying back and forth. Tommy was behind her, rubbing her shoulders. She touched her growing belly, pure rapture on her face. Pure contentment.

I had grown accustomed to these sudden flashes of intuition, of imagination, and I enjoyed the panorama before my closed eyes. Sometimes, I could even imagine I felt what Tommy and Jenny must have felt, so close was our connection.

Yes, their pregnancy was a brilliant time. A fulfillment of all their promises. A time of perfection. Jenny's diamond ring sparkled in the sunlight of the nursery. Tommy came to stand before her, slowly raising her hands to his lips.

Clasping the diary, I drifted between sleeping and waking. I cannot call it dreaming, for it was more like reality as the images of Tommy and Jenny's life played before my closed eyes like scenes from a movie.

The waves of bliss drifted over me, building and then subsiding, then building again. I felt as if someone had promised me a great surprise, but it was just beyond my reach to guess what it might be.

No matter. The joy was there. The promise of a child, the promise of a lifetime together.

Yes, I thought to myself, come back to me, Tommy.

Suddenly, a cry of pain escaped from my lips. The joy evaporated, leaving a naked terror and a pain so intense I doubled over in my bed. I curled into a ball like a frightened child, instantly awake.

I took a deep breath, not daring to move for fear the awful pain would return.

Waiting a moment, I seemed to be okay. I gave a cursory check to my body, wiggling my fingers and toes. Yes, everything still worked. The pain was gone. But, what in the world had happened to me?

Just then, another wave hit. An intense, crushing wave of pain rolled through my abdomen.

"Please, God, just let me wait for Tommy." The words escaped from my lips.

Tears squeezed from the corners of my eyes as the thoughts raced through my head. "What is going on?" I struggled. "Am I feeling Tommy's pain, Jenny's, or my own?"

I spoke out loud, "Take a deep breath. Calm down."

I breathed in. I breathed out.

I waited for another wave to hit, bracing myself for the blow of pain.

It did not come.

First one minute passed, then two, then ten.

Yes, I was okay — physically at least. But what had happened? Certainly, I was getting comfortable with the spontaneous images that played in my head, but that's all they were: images. They were a product of my imagination — a vivid imagination at that. Tommy's diary had become a story to me, a movie that played only in my head, to an audience of one.

This . . . this episode, or whatever you would call it, was something entirely different. This went beyond fantasy. The physical pain was real.

What was the connection? Those waves of pain had come to me from across time. They were not mine, yet they coursed through my body.

My hands trembled as I picked up the diary.

I was afraid the answer was in its pages.

I traced the worn leather cover with shaking fingers, thinking this was a bridge I could cross only once. If I found the answers here, inside this diary, I might never be the same again. I might be lost, forever, in the space between reality and imagination.

I opened the diary slowly, as if demons might escape if I were too hasty.

"Well," I tried to reassure myself, "maybe there's not much difference between imagining pictures and experiencing feelings."

That still didn't explain how I felt something I had never read.

But I couldn't give up. I had come too far.

I read the next few pages, the stark meaning of the words contrasting against the blurry, tear-stained ink.

No, I cried to myself. It can't be. Not now. They just began.

In an instant, it all made sense. The pain I had felt was Jenny's pain. Her cry for Tommy had escaped from my lips. It was incredible. My connection to this story, it seemed, was real.

"My God," I thought to myself, "I am either losing my mind or I have crossed the barrier of time. Perhaps what the old woman from the bookstore said was true: 'Love is all there is.'"

The love was still alive, I concluded. It was as if the universe was a fabric that wrinkled and overlapped, the threads of love reaching through from one age to the next, the lessons of one lifetime playing a vital role in another.

The feelings Tommy and Jenny shared were alive in these diary pages. They lived in the pristine air of Scotland. They lived in me.

I must know the whole story, I decided, beyond the solemn words in the diary. I was afraid, but I had to know. I only hoped I would not lose myself in the process.

"Well, you have always wanted to go where angels fear to tread," I thought to myself. It was time to put my faith in the ultimate good of this journey, to listen, once again, to the chant of my soul.

I closed my eyes. My body was still tightly clenched in a fetal position. "Come back to me, Jenny," I whispered. "I'm ready. Tell me your story."

❦

I saw, and felt, Jenny.

She lay drenched in sweat, the midwife sponging her forehead with a cool cloth.

"Jenny, dear, you must hold on. We've sent for Tommy. He'll help you through."

"This child must not die!" Jenny exclaimed. "I know it's a boy — our son. Please God, just let me wait for Tommy."

Jenny's body convulsed in pain, in another wave of labor. The midwife, unseen by Jenny, looked backwards, behind the bed, to the doctor. The question, unspoken, hung palpably in the air: Will she make it?

The doctor shook his head no. The hemorrhaging was too severe. Jenny had lost too much blood, and still the baby would not come.

"Hold on, Jenny," the midwife whispered. "You'll be all right — just wait for Tommy."

❧

Tommy was playing a challenge match at North Berwick that day, across the harbor from St. Andrews. His opponents: Willie and Mungo Park.

"You brothers are incorrigible! I'll beat you both. I promise to whip some sense into you," Tommy laughed on the first tee.

His playing partner was his father. They had accepted the challenge match even though the day was cold and windy.

Tommy had hesitated at first, but, as his father reminded him, Jenny had another two weeks to go before the birth. Surely a day or two apart could do no harm.

The Parks were among the top contenders for next year's Open, and Tom Morris, Sr. and Tom Morris, Jr. wanted to teach these cocky brothers a lesson.

The match was proceeding in high style. The Morrises won the first hole, the Parks the second. There was much laughter, as Willie Park exclaimed, "Young Tom — give your new son the same name, too, teach him to play golf, and I'll whip him just the way I'm whipping you!"

"Never in a million years, Willie Park. My son will grow up wearing my Championship Belt just to spite you!" Tommy exclaimed amid tears of laughter.

The merriment of play was interrupted by the head greenskeeper of North Berwick rushing out to meet the foursome on the fairway of the last hole.

"Young Tom! Young Tom! A telegram — it's urgent!"

Tommy raced to meet him. "Oh no," he thought silently, "Let it be anything but Jenny."

The words of the telegram were unmistakable:

YOUR WIFE SERIOUSLY ILL IN CHILDBIRTH.

STOP. COME AT ONCE. STOP.

Tommy's knees gave way. He gasped for breath, clutching the earth. "Not Jenny. Not Jenny," he repeated.

His father grabbed the telegram, read it, and shouted, "The train — get us to the train."

"But that's the problem, Mr. Morris," the greenskeeper cried. "The train has already left for today. We're stuck here until morning — we're virtually cut off from the world."

"Not if I can help it. My son must get to his wife. He must."

Willie Park broke in, "I . . . I have a boat, a small yacht really. It's more for pleasure sailing than for navigating rough waters, but it should make it across the bay. You can get a carriage from there."

Tommy's blue eyes flashed, locking Willie's gaze. "I'll take it. I have to get to Jenny. She'll be all right if I'm there. She can't leave me." His voice broke.

They raced to the edge of the bay together, Tommy leading the group. The boat was there. Tommy took several deep breaths before climbing in, stopping only to hug his father.

"She'll be fine, Dad. You'll see. Both her and the babe."

With Tommy inside the boat at the helm, his father untied the sloop, casting the rope onto the dock. The water was rough, but perhaps the strong wind would carry them quickly to the distant shore of St. Andrews.

"Godspeed, Tommy." The lone figures of Willie and Mungo Park retreated from Tommy's view as he sailed away. Away from North Berwick and toward Jenny.

～※～

"Tommy!" Jenny cried in agony.

"He's coming, dear. He'll be here any minute, just hold on. Take a deep breath, now . . . push."

Jenny pushed with all her might. "Tommy . . ." her voice echoed throughout the house.

"There's a good girl. You have a fine, handsome new son."

"Tommy, look, we have a son," Jenny was delirious now from the pain of childbirth and the severe loss of blood.

The midwife whispered to the doctor, "Will she make it?"

"It doesn't look good. Let's pray her husband gets here in time."

"Tommy," Jenny whispered. "I'm not afraid."

"Of course you're not, dear. You — both you and the baby — you'll be fine." The midwife wiped Jenny's brow again.

"Tommy . . . remember . . . love is all there is. From the light comes love. God, how I've loved you. I'll wait . . . forever, if I need to."

The midwife looked up, the worry and fear showing in her eyes. She held the tiny body of the child out to the doctor.

❦

Finally, Tommy reached the shoreline, jumping out into the water, wading the final yards to freedom . . . to Jenny. He collapsed on the sand, his body jerking with spasms, exhausted.

The harbormaster ran to meet him, clutching a thin yellow slip of paper. Another telegram.

"Thank God!" Tommy exclaimed. "She must be all right." He tore open the telegram, read the six solitary words that would change his life, and sank into the sand. The tears would no longer come. He was numb.

He could not breathe, and he did not want to.

The yellow telegram fluttered to the ground.

There, the words seems to etch themselves into the sand:

REGRET, YOUR WIFE HAS DIED. STOP.

❦

The tears that would not come to Tommy came to me. They flowed hot and bitter down my face.

12

A BLAZE OF GLORY

"HOW COULD GOD BE SO CRUEL AS TO TAKE JENNY AWAY from Tommy just as their life together had begun?" I railed.

The love Tommy had unlocked inside of me now flowed out in tears. What was the point of loving so deeply, I wondered, if only to risk losing again, this time to death?

I could not believe Jenny was gone. I remembered, of course, from my first introduction to Tommy's story that Jenny had died in childbirth. But somehow, feeling it now, feeling the love, it was not just Tommy's loss, it was mine.

I ate my breakfast in silence. I dressed solemnly.

I knew what I had to do. I would follow what surely must have been Tommy's footsteps in the days and weeks after Jenny's death. I would find her grave, and I would mourn with him.

Jenny was buried in the old cathedral churchyard, close to the spot where she and Tommy had become engaged.

I walked between the tangle of headstones, seemingly knowing where to find Jenny's grave.

The churchyard was quiet now. There were no mourners; there was no sound. Even the wind was silent in reverence to the felled majesty of Tommy and Jenny's love.

Her grave lay flat, directly next to Tommy's own large memorial stone.

I looked at the dates.

Jenny was barely two years younger than Tommy. Her stone was engraved 1875, the year her soul left the earth.

Her grave was not marked by a traditional headstone. Rather, Tommy had covered the entire breadth of her coffin with a heavy slab of marble. The marble still lay there, stoically covering her mute form from the sun.

A large cross was etched in the stone, and a heavy scrolled inscription lay at the top. It read:

Jenny Morris, beloved wife of Tommy
Laid here, 1875
Love is all that is left of the language of paradise
— Bulwer-Lytton
You taught me well, Jenny
I saw Eden, if only for an instant

My heart broke at the sight of the inscription. Tommy's pain seeped between every line. How alone he must have felt, ordering that slab of marble, choosing his final words to Jenny.

I sank to the ground in reverence for Jenny, carefully placing the bunches of heather I had brought in her honor, 120 years too late.

"Why, Jenny?" I asked. "Why did you leave so soon? Surely a love as great as yours and Tommy's must have had more importance."

Tears streamed silently down my cheeks. I looked from her grave to Tommy's, standing directly to my left. Tommy's memorial stone was nearly six feet tall. It stood over Jenny as though protecting her, sheltering her even in death.

Tommy's stone was arched with a beautiful sculpture

emerging from the marble. It was Tommy's likeness, bent over his golf club, wearing his Scots bonnet.

I looked to the other side of Jenny's grave for their child's. There was nothing.

I searched the entire churchyard, looking at every child's grave. There was simply nothing.

I returned, perplexed, to Jenny's grave and sat at the edge of Tommy's memorial stone, surrounded once again by the two lovers. I opened my daypack and extracted Tommy's diary, hoping to soothe my grief. There was, however, no emotion left in the diary. He had not written in it for nearly two months after Jenny's death.

Page after page was blank. I flipped through them mindlessly.

The emptiness of the diary spoke louder than words.

Tommy, I knew, was adrift without Jenny. Perhaps he had turned to drinking. Perhaps he simply sat alone in their house, day after day, mourning in darkness.

No matter what he did with his time, though, I was certain I knew how he must have felt.

"Why have you left me, Jenny?" he would cry. "You always said love is everything. It is not anymore. There is nothing but darkness. The light is no more."

Flipping the empty pages of the diary once more, I felt the darkness too. Had it engulfed Tommy? Was this how he had died, smothered by the longing?

And then, there was a spark from the diary pages.

It was a jolt, small but distinct, much like the electric feelings I had experienced when I first learned how Tommy and Jenny had met on the Old Course beach.

I looked down at the diary and turned the page.

A new sheet was filled with Tommy's familiar hand. As I read, I let the scenes unfold in my mind.

November 19, 1875

A short time before her death, Jenny told me something which haunts me still. Perhaps she meant to give me a clue. She said we had just begun to discover the power love can bring into our lives.

Love transcends the laws of nature, she said. What seems impossible, when done with love, is not only possible, but probable.

I learned this time and again with my golf.

She said our love would transcend the boundaries of space and time. Can it also transcend the boundaries of death? I must know.

Tommy looked up from the diary, the certainty of his decision dawning across his face. He became more sure with every word he wrote.

"I must try to reach Jenny, even if that means crossing the boundary of death itself," he concluded. "Our love is eternal. Jenny is not dead. Her spirit lives, and I can reach her. I know I can. If I can win any golf match in the world, if I can use love to transcend the laws of nature, I can surely be with my Jenny again."

Tommy flipped through the condolence cards on the table. They had been accumulating for two months, since Jenny's funeral in September.

Everyone urged him to play golf again.

They did not understand. He had no need to pick up a club. But now, as the idea formed in his mind, he flipped through the cards and found the one he wanted.

It was from Arthur Molesworth of Westward Ho!, the golf course in England his father had designed. Colonel Molesworth was the leading amateur there and also a most clever gambler.

Slicing open the envelope, Tommy read the card. He knew what Molesworth would say.

"What a pompous fool!" Tommy exclaimed. The card, as Tommy suspected, gave not only Molesworth's condolences on Jenny's death, it invited Tommy to a challenge match, ostensibly because golf would ease Tommy's grief.

"He wants to play me because he thinks my sorrow will affect my game," Tommy stated bluntly. "He wants to beat the great Tommy Morris, and he'll take any advantage he can."

Tommy opened his own correspondence folder and extracted a heavy, cream-colored card. It was embossed at the top: "Mr. and Mrs. Tom Morris, Jr." Jenny had ordered the stationery shortly after their wedding, so proud was she of their formal name.

Tommy traced the raised paper with his finger.

"For you, Jenny," he whispered. "I will prove to you that our love conquers all. Our love is here in my heart. I can use it to win, anytime, anyplace. I will leave this life in a blaze of glory, a blaze in your honor."

Tommy raised his ink pen, etching his reply to Arthur Molesworth in bold, black strokes.

In his note, Tommy accepted the challenge. Molesworth could set the amount — the higher, the better, he wrote. They would play six rounds of twelve holes per round, winner take all. Tommy gave him handicap strokes, an edge of six strokes per round, thirty-six strokes total. The only provision was that the match would have to be played immediately, before Christmas.

Tommy laughed.

Molesworth would surely accept his conditions. He would think Tommy had lost his mind. Not only was Tommy letting Molesworth set the bet, he was giving him handicap strokes. Tommy would start each round of competition with a score of six. Molesworth would start with zero. The final low score would win.

"This should be very interesting," Tommy said as he sealed the envelope.

The match between Tommy and Molesworth was set at the Royal North Devon Golf Club, Westward Ho!, in England, a fortnight later.

Tommy had not played golf since Jenny died, not even to practice.

Winter came upon England harsh and cold that December.

The umpire for the match wanted to call the game off. After all, the greens were completely covered with snow. But Arthur Molesworth was not about to let Tommy out of their challenge so easily. He was not going to give up his unusual advantage. Tommy might change his mind if they waited until the spring.

"No," Molesworth declared. "The greens will have to be swept."

And so, the first day of competition was spent not in play but in clearing each green of snow, every green of the entire twelve-hole course.

The second day, Tommy and Molesworth began to play.

Tommy stood at the first tee of the course his father had designed in 1864. It was the first formal golf course to be built in England, a seaside links like the best golf courses in Scotland.

"There is a sense of limitless freedom about this course," Tommy thought. It was very similar to Carnoustie, where Tommy had won his first professional tournament.

Walking the course the day before, Tommy had familiarized himself with the crazy patchwork quilt of holes his father had designed. Many of them crossed over one another. If another pair of golfers had been in play that day, their balls would have whizzed over Tommy's head.

By the time he teed off on the first hole, Tommy knew how he would play every hole.

He would play with love. He would play with intuition.

He did not need to practice. He would simply release the fear and let the love rush in, as Jenny had taught him.

Tommy turned to Arthur Molesworth as they began their first round. Blue eyes flashing, Tommy predicted, "I will not only win your money today. I will show you that love, not pride, wins golf matches. My play today is for my wife, Jenny."

Molesworth did not quite know how to respond.

Tommy's words disturbed him. It was as if Tommy did not realize Jenny was dead.

"No matter," Molesworth thought. "I will take this advantage. If Tommy is insane, so be it. He is still the great Tommy Morris, and sane or insane, it will be a feather in my cap to beat him."

"Let's play," Molesworth replied.

The first hole was a 478 yard par-five, shorter than the par-fives Tommy usually played.

Tommy decided to make the hole in four strokes.

He did, of course.

"Molesworth," Tommy concluded as they walked toward the next tee box, "I will venture to say I will birdie every hole today. Such is the power of my love."

Molesworth simply shook his head. The man was mad.

Near the end of their first round, Tommy was ahead by six strokes, despite Molesworth's handicap advantage.

The two men stepped up to the eleventh hole, 398 yards long, a par-four. It was bounded and intersected by a wilderness of sea rushes, apparently left over from when the ocean originally claimed the land. The rushes were in such a position that you first had to drive your ball over them, and then avoid them with your second shot if you were to continue up the fairway. One wayward shot and you would be trapped by the bushy undergrowth.

Tommy loved the course. Every challenge was an invitation to prove his skill, an invitation to prove his love.

He lined up his tee shot, pulled back, and impacted with the ball. His shaft snapped in two.

"Another club lost," Tommy muttered to himself.

Molesworth stood in awe.

Tommy's shot landed far beyond the treacherous rushes, only 120 yards from the green. He would easily make his birdie on this hole.

Tommy stood above the ball and pulled his niblick from his bag. "This is my favorite golf shot," he thought.

It was the shot for which he was famous. Tommy had learned, many years earlier, how to impart backspin on a golf ball. Few golfers had mastered the technique as Tommy had. He could strike the ball in such a way that it would rotate backwards as it flew toward its destination. In this way, when the ball hit the ground, it would bite and stick. It allowed Tommy to place his shots precisely, particularly on fast or sloping greens.

Tommy's unusual ability came in handy during the competition at Westward Ho! On this wintry day, greens cleared of snow, the grass was still frozen. It was as slick as ice. Golf balls, when shot without backspin, would hit the frozen green and slide — often ending up twenty or thirty feet beyond the point of impact.

Not Tommy's ball, however. Tommy hit his second shot and put the ball just two feet from the cup. It impacted, spun backward, and rolled into the cup.

He had made an eagle on this par-four hole.

"I just picked up another two strokes," Tommy called back to Molesworth, who was by now regretting his decision to play in the snow.

By the end of the competition two days later, Tommy and Arthur Molesworth had played seventy-two holes of golf. Tommy bested him six rounds out of six. Not only did Tommy win, his margin was an amazing fifty-one strokes. The match was a thrashing.

There had never been a finer display of Tommy's power. If the world had any doubt about who the greatest golfer was, Tommy reminded them.

Love always wins.

Jenny's love did not die with her body. It was left behind.

It was there for Tommy to access at any time.

Spectators watching the match remarked that Tommy seemed to be the player of old, the man who many years before had won Open championship after Open championship.

One sports writer, up from London to watch the match, wrote, "I cannot imagine anyone playing better than Young Tommy."

Old Tom was the happiest of all, thinking his son had returned to the living. They would play golf together again, Old Tom reasoned, for Tommy was back.

But he was not.

After the competition, in the safety of his home, Tommy reflected on his admiring fans: "I hope they saw the majesty. This competition was for Jenny. It proves, one last time, that love is not just a feeling, but a way of living."

Tommy returned to his diary, etching his final words.

December 8, 1875

I know what I must do now. For so long, I was drifting without Jenny. My love had no place to go. At first, I thought it was the loss of her love that pained me so. After all, she warmed me each day with the force of her very being.

But I was wrong. The pain came from the love I did not give.
I closed my heart when Jenny died. I no longer gave her my love.
My love stayed trapped inside of me.

I will open my heart to her again. I will open my heart to
transcend the boundary of time. I now believe we will be together
again.

13

CHRISTMAS TOGETHER

TOMMY'S BODY AGED RAPIDLY BEFORE EVERYONE'S EYES. OVER the next few weeks, his hair turned white like an old man's. He shuffled through his daily chores, his joints no longer agile. He grew winded from even short walks along the beach.

It was as though his physical body realized it was no longer needed to contain his spirit. It was an unnecessary vessel; the essence of his soul would soon depart.

On Christmas Eve, three months after Jenny's death, Tommy was visited by his father and closest friends.

As they approached the whitewashed cottage from the

shore road, they saw that the house was dark. Tommy's Christmas tree, identical to the tree Jenny had decorated the previous year, stood unlit in the window.

Twilight was approaching, but no lanterns burned in Tommy's house.

Old Tom led the small group to the rear of the house, to the picnic clearing Tommy had created for Jenny. The view of the beach from this angle was magnificent. When she was alive, it was the spot Jenny had most loved. It was where Tommy now spent his days.

The sight that the small group beheld was heartbreaking.

Tommy was sitting in Jenny's wicker rocker. He was wrapped in blankets, a rug spread across his lap as though he were an invalid. He stared blankly at the sea, his white hair ruffled by the wind.

He did not look like Tommy at all.

Old Tom spoke first, clearing his throat to break the awkward silence. "Son, we've come to visit. We've brought you Christmas dinner. It's na' good for you to stay here alone. Come inside with us now."

Tommy did not stir.

Old Tom continued. "Your friends are here. I'm here. I know you're grieving, but ye have to rejoin the living. Celebrate

Christmas with us."

Tommy spoke without emotion, without ever turning his head. "I am alive, Father. I am with Jenny. She and I are part of something much bigger than ourselves. Our love is the only reality. It is the beginning and the end, the death and the birth. You do not understand where I am. You cannot understand where I am going."

Not a single muscle twitched as Tommy spoke. He did not move. His eyes never turned away from his focus on the beach.

The small party of well-wishers shifted awkwardly, looking from one another to Tommy and back again.

John Inglis, the judge who had married Tommy and Jenny, spoke next, trying to break Tommy's transfixed gaze. "I've known you for many years, Tommy. Through good times and now through bad. Open your heart to us again. Open your heart to life."

Tommy turned, slowly. He looked at John as if hearing his native language for the first time. "My heart *is* open. Can't you see? Jenny's death did not close my heart; only I can do that. I am here, now, opening it to her again."

"Then come inside wi' us, Tommy. Share our Christmas dinner," Old Tom interjected.

Tommy leaned forward, silently wondering if he should join his father and friends, or return to the sanctity of his mind.

He paused, and then clutched the rocker's arms as leverage to lift his weary body. He would join the group, he decided, for a short time, to make them happy.

John darted forward to give Tommy a hand.

As he grasped Tommy's arm, Tommy leaned forward and whispered, "Jenny died so she would die no more."

In that instant, John knew what Tommy meant to do. Tommy had quoted an American philosopher, Herman Hooker. With those brief words, John knew that Tommy meant to join Jenny in eternity, and that, most likely, within a week's time he would preside over his best friend's funeral.

Strangely, though, he realized he should not try to stop Tommy. He did not understand his choice and could not fathom the courage it would take to reach into the black chasm of death. But, somehow, in spite of his own fear, John sensed this was a divine plan he should not interrupt.

He would enjoy the evening together with his friend, their last evening.

Tommy broke the spell that had woven them together in silence. "It is all right, John. We have tonight. And you will remember the love."

John helped Tommy inside, shouldering the frail weight of his body. The others followed, awed and touched by the sight of the two men leaning together, stepping carefully through the sand to the kitchen door.

In spite of the empty chair at the end of the table, Jenny's chair, the evening was gay.

Tommy lit the candles on the Christmas tree and illuminated every lantern in the house. The rooms were ablaze with friendship.

Together, they ate the turkey dinner Old Tom had brought, drank toasts of Scotch whisky to the next year's golfing season, and sang Christmas carols. As midnight neared, Tommy rose from his chair and lifted his glass.

"This is an evening as Jenny would have wanted," Tommy toasted. "She loved you all, as I do. Christmas is a time of forgiveness and of peace. Remember me thus."

Tommy gulped his drink and shuffled toward his bedroom, leaving his guests bewildered at the dining room table.

One by one, they rose to leave, blowing out the candles and dousing the lanterns.

"I'll come for ye in the morning, Tommy," his father called to the silent house.

Tommy did not hear his father's final words.

He had retreated into his mind, once again.

Tommy stood before the looking-glass in his bedroom and absently brushed his hair. He tucked a loose strand of wavy hair behind his ear, smoothing the curls. He slowly changed into his pajamas, choosing the blue-striped bottoms Jenny had sewn for him just a month before her death. His chest was bare.

He lay down on their marriage bed and remembered how it felt to curl behind Jenny's warm body.

He stretched his hand across the bed. It was cold now.

Tommy closed his eyes, and repeated the lessons of love he had learned since Jenny's death.

It has been three months now. I have so much to share with you, so much to tell. But you know all of this now, don't you. You are knowledge itself.

When you died, I thought the door to our love had closed. But I have learned from your absence that love never dies. Death is not a barrier to love. There are no boundaries or barriers to love.

I believe, Jenny, that our love was for a greater purpose. Your death has shown me that love transcends reason. Love transcends physical reality and thus makes all things possible.

This is why you died. To teach me this final lesson. To teach others, as well. Only the body is claimed by death. When our spirit has been healed by love, we have no need for our body. We can return to God.

Our love healed one another, Jenny. It will heal others too. I will leave the message of our love behind, on earth, to show others through our example.

This is my legacy; it is captured in this diary. I leave it for anyone who has eyes to see. I go to heaven now with your hand in mine. Our story, our love, will live on.

Tommy's heart grew still, his breathing slowed. Slower and yet even slower.

And then without warning, without commotion, his heart simply stopped.

His pain turned into rapture.

Tommy was soaring. He was instantly a seagull swooping across the beach. He was the cathedral ruins, a mute stone boulder lying on the grass. He was a tree, reaching for sunlight. He was everything, and he was nothing.

He felt every sensation of physical reality. He tasted sweet sugar cane, he felt a sharp thorn prick his finger, he saw the burning orange of a sunset. Every sensation was alive, but not contained.

It was limitless. He was limitless.

And then, through the soft mists, he felt Jenny.

He smelled her scent; he felt the crush of her weight in his arms. He was with her.

"Hello," she said. "I've been waiting."

And it was again, as always, Tommy and Jenny.

14

LOVE'S SECRET REVEALED

SNUGGLED IN THE SHADOW OF TOMMY'S MEMORIAL STONE, I closed the diary for the final time, my face warmed by the certainty of Tommy and Jenny's reunion.

It was not what I had expected.

The strength of Tommy and Jenny's love amazed me. Jenny's death, Tommy's loneliness without her — it had all been transformed by the purity of their love. Her death was a resurrection, not a final ending.

Suddenly, the lessons of Jenny's death came to me, as they had come to Tommy.

"Love is eternal," I declared. "Love is all there is. Pain, fear, longing, desire — in the end it is all transformed into love."

I stroked the cover of the diary.

"Thank you, Tommy, for this legacy. Thank you for this message."

My heart was lighter than it had ever been. I felt the joyful abandon of a child, as if the mystery and mirth of the world was mine once more.

I felt the wisdom of ancient memories guiding me with a gentle hand. Now I knew how to proceed in life, how to release the love inside me.

Love's secret, I realized, was paradoxical. To receive great love, you first have to give great love. And to give great love, you must find it within your heart to love not just one person, but everyone and everything — all of life: one's work, as Tommy loved his golf; one's family, as Tommy loved his wife and father.

I thought how radically my life would change if I consciously chose the path of love, if I chose to love everyone and everything, all the time.

I thought of a million expressions of love: a kind word, a compliment, a smile. I laughed a quiet chuckle, which deepened into peals of joy.

The love I longed for was inside me all along.

It was time to give my love to the world. I would no longer worry about *being* loved; I would simply focus on *loving*.

I looked at the diary and realized how difficult it would be to return this book to its owner. The diary had become my trusted friend and companion. It had become my guide.

The end of the circle was drawing near.

I looked across to Jenny's grave and then back up at Tommy's. The stones no longer seemed cold, but warmed by love.

As I stood up, the diary slipped from my hands, tumbling behind me. I reached for it and noticed another prominent gravestone, set slightly behind Tommy's.

It was Old Tom's.

Curious, I stepped up to the marble obelisk. It was engraved with the year of Old Tom's death: 1908.

"You continued to play golf after Tommy's death, didn't you?" I queried the hushed stone. "You had a heavy heart, I know. All you wanted in life was to play with Tommy again. But you never really understood the power of his love."

Then, a sudden flash of intuition blinded me.

It made sense now. The absence of a child's small grave made sense.

"Tommy's son did not die," I realized, incredulously. "That's why there is no grave for the baby."

The accusation in my tone grew. "You never told Tommy his son lived, did you, Old Tom? You thought it would be easier if Tommy made a clean break — if he mourned once and moved on. You thought the child would remind Tommy every day of his loss of Jenny. How wrong you were. Control only stifles love. By attempting to control his life, you lost Tommy forever."

I shook my head. "You may have been the grandfather of golf, Old Tom, but you were a fool."

I turned to Tommy's stone in reverence. With regret and longing for what might have been, what father and son might have shared, I traced the outline of Tommy's memorial with my finger.

Slowly, I realized that it was time to leave Tommy. It was time to return the diary to the bookstore.

Dusk was fast approaching. "Another cold evening in St. Andrews," I thought, as I gratefully tugged on my sweater.

I left the graveyard and found my way to the bookstore.

This time, though, I noticed every detail. I saw the curved front window, the books on display, the heavy leaded glass of the front door.

A blue light flashed from the window, sparking my attention.

I looked and saw it hanging there, in the center of the display window. It was the cobalt blue blown-glass suncatcher Tommy gave Jenny upon the celebration of her pregnancy.

Bright blue shadows from the suncatcher reflected on the far wall of the bookstore turning the final rays of sunshine into a brilliant spectacle. It must have cast this same color on the walls of Jenny's nursery.

I marveled at the sight.

"This treasure was here all along," I thought to myself, "and I did not notice."

I opened the door, cowbells clanging.

The elderly clerk nodded to me in recognition, a smile slowly dawning across her face. "You've discovered Tommy and Jenny's secret." There was no question in her tone. "It is written on your face."

I looked at her in amazement.

"Oh, of course I know what is in the diary. Why do you think it is here on the shelves, instead of in a dusty museum?" Her soft face puckered with unspent laughter.

"You've read it then? You've read the diary?" I asked.

"The diary has always been here. It has been waiting to reveal the secrets of love."

"Then there have been others?" I questioned. "Others who came before me?"

The old woman puzzled for an instant, her brow clenched in disappointment, then smoothing again with hope. She spoke slowly. "Others have come, but you are the first person to accept the challenge. The others came into the store. They picked up the diary, even read a few pages. But they all put it back on the shelf."

I was softly, silently amazed. "Oh," I breathed.

"Everyone waits for love to come to them," she continued. "Very few people come to love."

My thoughts, my feelings, the lessons I had learned — they came together in an instant. I wanted to share my experiences with the elderly clerk, to deepen our connection.

My heart poured out its discoveries, seeking intimacy. "Reading this diary was a journey of love," I began. "The love between Tommy and Jenny has been an awakening for me. I don't think I ever really knew how to love before now. Somehow, this diary, this legacy of their love, was something I could not resist.

"Now, if only I could find someone who understands the secret of true love," I said. "Someone to love and to share this knowledge with."

The old woman smiled. "When you know how to love, your love shines on others. This will draw your beloved to you.

"Every life, every desire of our heart has a purpose," she said. "When you are ready to accept your destiny, your beloved will appear. He will also know how to love, and you will instantly recognize one another."

My eyes clouded with tears, tears of happiness, of anticipation. She was right, I knew.

"The suncatcher," I blurted, pointing to the blue glass disk suspended in the front window. "It's Tommy and Jenny's. How did it get here?"

"You must have realized by now that their child did not die."

I nodded.

"The Morris family still lives in St. Andrews," she continued. "Tommy's son lived until 1950. I knew him myself when I was a young girl. Like his father, he longed for love. In fact, each one, each generation, has been waiting for a love like Tommy shared with Jenny. The diary has been here, on the bookshelves, waiting for someone to continue the journey Tommy and Jenny started."

She paused and seemed to notice my physical presence for the first time. She took in the sight of my worn sweater drooping lifelessly over slim hips, the brown of my hair. It was not curly like Jenny's, but straight and fine.

She looked bluntly into my eyes. "I knew what would happen when someone truly came for the diary," she said.

I raised my eyebrow in a silent question.

"Everything has been leading to this one moment in time," she answered, her face radiant with hope. "The circle closes, only to begin again."

She abruptly turned from me, disappearing behind the bookstacks. In the distance, I could hear her speak to someone I could not see.

"She has returned with the diary," I heard her say.

Footsteps approached, heavy steps, a man's steps.

A deep voice resonated, and I felt a ringing in my soul.

My heart leapt as the man came into clear view. He was lean and strong, softness and power coiled in every step. The waves of his soft brown hair were tucked behind one ear.

His first words were intimate and deeply felt. They continued an unspoken conversation, answering my thoughts.

"I learned about love when I first read the diary," he began. "I knew if I lived each day with love in my heart, as purely and simply as Tommy did, one day someone would come."

I looked deeply into the vivid blue of his eyes and realized I had seen that particular shade of blue only once before — in my visions of Tommy.

Ancient memories slowly dawned on me as I reached forward to clasp his outstretched hand.

"Hello," I affirmed, stepping forward to meet my destiny.

He smiled broadly, understanding, knowing, taking my hand in his.

"I am Tommy Morris," he said, as I knew he would.

A Word From the Author

I WROTE *THE LEGEND OF TOMMY MORRIS* AS A TRIBUTE TO MY brother, Jeffrey, who was killed in a car accident in 1993.

When Jeff died, I was haunted with regrets about the words I did not say and the love I did not show him. I had always reasoned that Jeff was difficult to love, but now, with his death, I could not shake the feeling that somehow, I had failed him.

In the months that followed, I searched for a way to express my grief. In an interesting coincidence, I was shown a golf book with a brief mention of Tommy Morris, Jr., who became famous in Scotland not only for his outstanding golfing achievements, but for his passionate love for his wife. It said Tommy had died of a broken heart.

I, too, knew what it was like to have my heart constrict with longing, to desperately want to be reunited with someone I loved.

I immediately saw the parallels between Tommy's life and the answer I was searching for. Hidden between the historical details of Tommy's brief life was the spirit and meaning of what he had left behind: the spirit of true love.

As I wrote this book, I started to live Tommy's principles of love — becoming aware of love's presence and choosing love above all else. I discovered that love is a choice. It does not matter who is right or who is wrong. It matters that we love. During this time, miracles began to abound in my life. My long-strained relationship with my father was healed as I, and he, chose love over anger and fear. I was also reunited with other family members in a bond of healing. I discovered that the more love I gave, the more love came to me.

It is my deepest wish that through these pages, Tommy will show you how to find love as well.

If you long for love, if you grieve the loss of a relationship, if you mourn the death of a loved one, then it is you for whom I have written this book.

The love Tommy shared with Jenny is meant to be yours. Love is your destiny. You are meant to love and be loved with the full power of your soul.

Love can, and does, transcend the laws of time and space. Love is not bound by this world. *Love is all there is.*

I welcome you to share your thoughts and feelings with me.

Anne Kinsman Fisher
P.O. Box 10024
Savannah, GA 31401

Email: WriteTommy@aol.com

ACKNOWLEDGMENTS

ALTHOUGH ONLY THE AUTHOR'S NAME APPEARS ON THE FRONT cover, a book is a cumulative expression of love.

I wish to thank the many souls who shared this journey with me, whose generous spirits are reflected within these pages:

My mother and father, Mary Anne and Bob Thomas

My father, Robert Kinsman Fisher

My dear friends, Brian and Cecelia Fradet

And those who prayed for this project and for me:
Karen Bouvier, Suzan Woods, Mary Rose Busby, Ken Justice, Rev. Margee Grounds, and my spiritual family at Unity of Savannah. Your faith in me was unwavering, and thus made this book possible.

And finally, to the woman whose tender care, nurturing, and abundant love made *Tommy* what he is today, Janet Mills. I am honored to call you editor and friend.

The Seven Spiritual Laws of Success by Deepak Chopra
In this classic international bestseller, Deepak Chopra distills the essence of his teachings into seven simple, yet powerful principles that can easily be applied to create success in all areas of our lives.

Child of the Dawn by Gautama Chopra
A rich and colorful parable about a young boy's search for meaning and empowerment. Based on the principles from his father's book, *The Seven Spiritual Laws of Success,* this engaging tale is guaranteed to enchant and inspire readers of all ages for generations to come.

Creating Affluence by Deepak Chopra
With clear and simple wisdom, Deepak Chopra explores the full meaning of wealth consciousness and presents simple A-to-Z steps that spontaneously generate wealth in all its forms.

The Crescent Moon by Deepak Chopra (Audio Cassette)
This audio celebrates the tender innocence of childhood and the joyous, simple pleasures of living. Deepak Chopra captures the warmth and spirit of Rabindranath Tagore's prose poetry, as sounds of nature and the inspiring flute of G. S. Sachdev grace our listening experience.

Living Without Limits by Deepak Chopra and Wayne Dyer
(Audio Cassette) Two leaders in the field of human potential share their wisdom before a live audience as they question and challenge one another on the importance of quieting the inner dialogue, the power we have to heal ourselves of fatal diseases, the negative impact of the media on our health, and more.

The Nature of Personal Reality by Jane Roberts
In this perennial bestseller, Seth challenges our assumptions about
the nature of reality and stresses the individual's capacity for conscious
action.

Seth Speaks by Jane Roberts
One of the most powerful of Jane Roberts' "Seth Books," this essen-
tial guide to conscious living clearly and powerfully articulates the
furthest reaches of human potential, and the concept that we all
create our own reality.

The Individual and the Nature of Mass Events by Jane Roberts
Extending the idea that we create our own reality according to our
beliefs, Seth explores the connection between personal beliefs and
world events.

The Nature of the Psyche by Jane Roberts
Seth reveals a startling new concept of self, answering questions
about the real origins and incredible powers of dreams, human sex-
uality, and how we choose our physical death.

The "Unknown" Reality, Volumes One and Two by Jane Roberts
Seth explains how understanding unknown dimensions can change
the world as we know it. A fascinating exploration of the interde-
pendence of multiple selves, the purpose of dreams, the relationship
between physical health and inner reality, and more.

The Oversoul Seven Trilogy by Jane Roberts
One of the most imaginative tales ever written, the adventures of
Oversoul Seven are at once an intriguing fantasy, a mind-altering
exploration of our inner being, and a vibrant celebration of life.